THE BLUES FOR ANNIE MAE

D.J. PARHAMS

Wasteland Press
Shelbyville, KY USA
www.wastelandpress.net

The Blues For Annie Mae
by D.J. Parhams

Second Printing – November 2007
ISBN: 978-1-60047-145-2
Illustration done by Luis A. Limardo

Printed in the U.S.A.

This book is dedicated to the loving memory of my mother,
Jannie Mae Parhams-Chew.

Acknowledgements

They say it takes a village to raise a child. Sometimes, it also takes a village to publish a book. The following names are all a part of my village and I thank them immensely.

Luis Limardo
Mel Levitino
Dinah "Sheena" Hoover
Ina Jackson
Betty Donnerson-Rembert
Raphael T. Powell
Mana Lesman-Sewert
Tim Veeley
Connie Kiosse
Vicki Austin
Craig Erving
David Chew
C. "Lamar" Snell
Janet Williams
Nancy Beckett
George Michael

Part I

1986

WHOOSH…WHOOSH…WHOOSH…"I'll pick gravel in HELL before I stand up and let you fuck over me!" she shouts.

Mrs. Selma Louise Jenkins has grabbed hold of the broom and is whacking me upside the head with it.

WHOOSH… "Don't you…ever…come…up… in…heah…" WHOOSH… dis…respecting,"… WHOOSH… "me…" WHOOSH… "and… disrespecting…" WHOOSH "my…house…" WHOOSH! I try to run, but the bristles get tangled up in my hair.

"Turn me loose," I scream. "Turn me loose!"

"Oh, I'll turn yo ass loose alright." And Mama gets a good grip on that broom handle and slams her foot into my back. She sends me hurling down the hallway. Now, I'm determined not to hit the floor, so my body is doing a herky-jerky dance to stay afloat. Because I know once I'm down there on that floor, Mama's going to have a prayer meeting on my behind. WHOOSH…WHOOSH, she's at me again. I take off, like the devil from Holy Water. That broom is steadily singing in the breeze and pounding down on my back. WHOOSH…WHOOSH! At this point I'm so busy running, and screaming and looking back at Mama; I'm not watching where I'm going. I can feel the straws of the broom cutting and scraping into my skin, like steel wool to a pot. And I don't even notice that one of her rugs is rumpled up in the living room…until I trip over it…BOOM. For a moment it seems as if I'm suspended in mid-air. Desperately, my hands grope for thin air. Mama helps the situation along with a powerful WHOOP of the broom handle upon my back. I crash down to the floor with a cruel thump, and I land in a perfect 'T' formation.

And Mama is whipping me with that broom as if her very life depends on it!

WHOOSH…WHOOSH…WHOOSH…after each whoosh my body jumps and vibrates and her heavy breaths floats above me. After each breath she pants and sighs like a dying animal. At this point I hear another pair of footsteps running up behind me. It's my sister Gloria, she grabs the broom in mid-air and screams, "Don't hit her anymore Mama! Pleeze don't hit her!"

You see, it isn't Gloria's place to stop Mama from whipping me. I want her to whip me for all of the wrong I've done. I want her to whip all the pain away…gashes and lashes of pain. They're both in back of me now and I just lay here and stare at the wiggly, flowery shapes on the red rug.

My truth has me locked to this floor. And all I can do is lay here and look at the flower pattern on the rug. And I feel as if these very flowers are unhinging themselves and they're swirling and twirling all around me. And my mind unhinges itself too and swirls and twirls with the flowers and it dog-paddles back in to time, gathering up threads from the past at a lightning speed. And I remember, I remember who I was, and how I was.

Circa 1962

"Breathe Baby" Mama howls. "Take yo time and breathe, Sugar. Don't let nobody rush you!" And Mama clasps her hands and puffs out a proud sigh and says, "Oooohhh, you just wait and see, my Baby is gonna be somebody one day. My Baby is gonna be the next Marianne Anderson or the next Leotyne Price! That's MY baby up there on that stage." Mama says, boasting to the near-by people in the audience. And they all smile their little polite smiles and turn their attention back to the stage. I guess Mama forgets that they are parents too. And like all parents they too have dreams and aspirations for their children.

And I stand on the stage with wobbly seven-year-old legs making a grand effort to tap dance while my wobbly nervous voice sings, *"ZIPPITY DOO DAH"*. I can't really see the audience because I have this bright light shinning in my face, but I can hear Mama shouting out directions, "Emote Baby, don't forget to emote! Turn! Don't forget your turns!"

I can feel my wavy black curls bouncing against my shoulders and the stiffness of my blue and white dress with an even stiffer, itchy petticoat, scratching against my legs and knees with my every move.

Mama, with her drill sergeant self, had me rehearse my big finish over and over again, the part where I go down on one knee and my arms open wide and I smile my cutesy smile. Well, sure enough, it comes time for my big finish and I rock it and sock it and knock them dead. Well…I knock them dead alright…when my hands extend so does a fart. I'm talking about a BIG BEHIND fart. The fart of all farts! And it seems to follow the flow of my hands. You know how a car sounds when it's being driven on a flat…PUPUPUPUPUPU? Well, that's how my fart sounds. And with the auditorium being so quiet and so vast, I think if they listen hard enough, they can hear that fart all the way down in Tupelo, Mississippi!

A mournful OHHHHHHH, stretches across the audience and bounces across the walls and zings and pings its way back to every crack and crevice of my embarrassment. I can't see Mama's eyes, but I can sure feel her eyes, sizzling into me like bacon in a skillet. I want to fly off that stage, but my feet won't let me. It feels like my feet have been shellacked to the floor boards. Finally, Ms. Havens, my second grade teacher comes out and peels my feet from the floor and carries me off that stage.

When me and Mama make it home that night, she won't even look at me. It's a long dreadful cord of silence and regret, a cord that Mama refuses to cut. I try to make conversation with Mama in my seven-year-old way. I try to make Mama laugh in my seven-year-old way, but she is so hurt and so embarrassed I think she feels that I did it out of spite. Mama wears a house coat of silence and a Velcro strip for a mouth, for days after that. It's as if Mama doesn't understand that I'm only seven years old …seven years old!

Growing up, my sister Gloria is a wild child. She has a boyfriend by the name of Arthur Legg. And they have that hot buttered kinda love for each other. Now, I know you know the kinda love I'm talking about, the kind of love that has to be savored any time anywhere. Now, I'm five years younger than my sister and it seems like every time I turn around, their tongues are doing a snake dance down each other's throat. That child would have married Arthur too, if Uncle Sam hadn't gotten hold of him. And like so many other boys at that time, he is drafted at eighteen and dead by nineteen.

Gloria gets THE call from Arthur's parents and they deliver that child a coffin of tears. And her body grows stiff, all except her arms and with vacant eyes and a quick wrist she knits and pearls, pearls and knits that very phone cord around her neck, tighter and tighter, twisting it into little knots. And when me and Mama try to undo the knots, "Let me dieeeee," she garbles. "Goddammit, let me dieeeee!"

Now, to this day, I don't know if Mama did it because Gloria has worked herself into a babbling frenzy, or because Gloria is cursing in her presence. Either way, Mama hauls off and slaps Gloria…And Lord, Lord what did she do that for?

Gloria's eyes grow as big as ping pong balls. And before you can say Ike and Tina Turner, she swoops down on Mama, like a vulture to a dead man! Now I thought that heifer was crazy when she was choking herself, but now I KNOW sister has lost her ever-lovin mind! She has Mama in a death grip. Our Mama, who will beat you down if you tell her, her eyes are black! Gloria is choking our Mama's neck while the phone is twisting and slinging from her own neck. Mama's eyes start to flutter and go into the back of her head. And her hands are slapping and flapping at the air. And Gloria is murmuring, "SHHHHHH, go to sleep…SHHHHH go to sleep!"

Now, I ain't about to slap Gloria, or do nothing stupid like that. I'm trying my best to get enough line on the phone so I can call 911! Gloria is so busy trying to send Mama to Glory she doesn't even notice that I'm calling the authorities on her nutso schizo behind.

After that, Gloria finds herself up in Thorazine heaven, courtesy of Reed Psychiatric Center, on the outskirts of Chicago. And she's kept drugged up and tied up for what seems like a long, long time. Finally, she's pronounced normal and sent home.

Oh, but you see, she isn't normal after that, not really normal. Wild child Gloria is gone. I think she dies somewhere, over in 'Nam with her lover man. And the new, so called normal Gloria becomes a second grade school teacher, living her second grade life. She never marries. She just teaches and stays at home with Mama, that's all.

Sometimes, I wonder, does she ever miss the juke joint life? You know what I'm talking about? I'm talking about standing in a darkened bar with a rum and coke in one hand and a fist full of problems in the other. Then the music starts juking from the juke box and you set your drink down and your problems down at the table. That's when the rhythm becomes your dance partner and the music takes you by the hand and you ride with the beat. You glide with the notes. You caress and collide all up and down and inside those G's and the B's and you realize the music becomes more than a dance partner, it becomes your lover. That's when your favorite part comes, and that's when the music hits that high, high crescendo, with that one last thump down, bump down beat and you raise up your arms and your head with a sho-nuf frown on your face and have mercy, you surrender…you surrender. When the song is gone and your lover has gone, you pick up your drink and your problems again and you perch against the bar and you wait and you wonder when will your new love come along? Will it be as good? Will it be as strong? So you wait to hear the clinking of the quarter rolling down inside the juke box once more.

I'll never forget the first time I sang for Mama. It's as fresh in my mind as peach cobbler in the oven. Oh, I couldn't be too much than 5-years-old at the time. I come bee-bopping into the kitchen and Mama is preparing vegetables for dinner. She's justa cut-cut-cutting and a chop-chop-chopping on the cutting board. I guess I get a hold of that beat and I start to singing, "AAA-A…BBB-B…CCC-C…" to Mama's knife drums and I spice it up with a little dance and prance. Mama drops that knife as if it's a murder weapon and rushes over towards me and she does it so fast that I'm thinking that I've done something wrong and that I'm in for the whipping of my life! She drops down before me, I search Mama's eyes to find out what it is that I've done so wrong. "Open yo mouth," she demands. She sucks in a deep breath of patience and says again, "Open yo mouth Baby. I just want to see something that's all," she says, with a smile and gentleness behind it.

Down south, some people believe that a person with a blessed voice has got to have a set of blessed tonsils to go along with it and that these tonsils are shaped and curved differently than most. Mama has her finger all down inside my mouth and just about her whole eyeball too. She's just a oohing and ahhing and carrying on something fierce, like she's found the Holy Grail down in there! "Open up wider Baby," she says. She probes and she jabs for a good five minutes and I'm about ready to puke and gag. I just KNOW that when I do, that Mama will beat me down like I stole sumptin. So I swallow it back down, the best I can.

And there's a change in Mama now. It's as if she's undergone some kinda grand metamorphosis. It's as if a veil has been lifted from Mama's face, a veil of non-commitment. She's no longer just a cliché housewife, serving her man, mothering her kids. She's a sister with a cause, a re-born woman. And there's a confident click in her heels, that wasn't there before. There's an erectness in Mama's back that wasn't there before. Mama's eyes hold a certain glint of self respect that wasn't there before. Being so young I can't imagine what has come over my mama. I'm not even sure if I like this new mama half as much as I liked the old one.

My days and nights are filled with school and lessons. After school each day I barely have time to put a thought in my head let alone a morsel in my mouth, before Mama is yanking me off to a voice lesson, tap lesson, or a ballet lesson.

And sometimes my legs are so achy and so stiff, I limp something awful. I sneak Mama's aspirin and ointment from the medicine cabinet. I never limp around Mama, because I 'm afraid of what she'll say…or do.

And Lord, Lord, Lord...there's Mama; at every lesson…there's Mama. With her pill box hat and white gloves on, there's Mama. Like a tree planted by the water, there's Mama. The other mothers help their children remove their little jackets and togs and would then remove themselves, but not MY MAMA! She plops herself down into a seat, like Alka Seltzer plops down into water.

Ms. Grey, my voice teacher is a bird-like little creature, with bird like little ways. She wears coke bottle glasses with her hair snatched into a severe little bun. Although she is quite young, she wears clothes that make her look much older and they all have these high, granny neck collars.

Well, I guess Ms. Grey rents a room in one of those music buildings downtown, over on Wabash Avenue somewhere. The first time me and Mama walk into the room, the only piece of furniture we see is this huge Baby Grand piano with the matching bench, surrounded by nothing but mirrors. Ms Grey sits at the bench with her hands folded, greeting us warmly and batting her eyes behind those coke glasses, and there isn't a chair to be found, and sure enough, Mama plops her behind right down on that bench, and pays Ms. Grey no mind. She forces that itty-bitty teacher to scoot over and make some room.

Mama sits there bobbing her already crossed legs, like she ain't got a care in the world. Ms. Grey looks at Mama like she'll cut her and gut her. Mama looks at Ms. Grey as if she'd serve her up for Sunday dinner. Ms. Grey politely clears her throat and proceeds with the lesson. You know and I know that from that day on there was always a folding chair sitting in the corner.

Do you know that not only does Mama have the emancipated gall to sit through every lesson, but whenever the notion hits her, she calls herself trying to TEACH that woman's class? Now, if I'm having trouble learning a breathing technique, Mama jumps up from her seat and brushes past that woman, like Christ passes up sin. Don't you think for one drip of a second that MY Mama would say excuse me…not in THIS lifetime! And she twists her behind over towards me and places her hand on my diaphragm and chest and with tiny slits for eyes she hisses, "You better breathe, and breathe right!"

Ms. Grey doesn't say nothing. That poor woman would just sit there and clear her throat and yank at those tight fitting collars and a couple of times I can swear I hear her gnashing her teeth. Mama does this at just about every other class too.

There are these four peculiar girls in my ballet class; I call them the Clone Sisters. They gather in a semi-circle near the edge of the room, away from the other students, with their blonde hair piled neatly upon their little heads, held tightly together by little pink bows. Their little pink tutus crown their narrow, little hips. Their fingers press against their little thin mouths as they haunch in their bony shoulders and giggle their little giggles, which are aimed directly at me and Mama.

Outside of the building, on our way to my next lesson, darkness creeps across the autumn sky and I complain to Mama about the Clone Sisters. Mama makes long effortless strides across the pavement; she holds her purse firmly at her side. She tosses her curls and flicks her bracelet clad wrist through the air and says, "Ta hell with 'em Honey. They don't mean you no-good. They ain't gonna give you nothing, but a hard way ta go."

Mama's attention is like red, sticky, sweet syrup that she's constantly pouring all over me. Sometimes, I feel that if I'm not careful that Mama will drown me in that very syrup. Sometimes I wonder, has she forgotten all about Daddy and Gloria? They're like two knick-knacks that sit in the corner and gather dust.

One night, through my walls I hear the dry, rifling sound of folding and unfolding papers. "What the fuck do you think you're doing Selma," asks Daddy in a low, hush tone.

"I'm trying to give my daughter a future. That's what the fuck I'm doing," answers Selma, not caring about her tone or volume.

"What about our future Selma, yours and mine?" and a long silence hangs in the air and permeates the walls.

Finally, after giving it much thought, Mama says "How can I have a future with a 'Ho chaser?" The silence that follows leaves a hollow imprint in my Daddy's favorite chair. A chair that remains empty for the rest of my childhood.

Well, I don't know about you or your household, but in mine on a Sunday morning, sick or well, by 8:30 you'd better be dressed and ready to give the Lord Jesus his praise, and if you even dream of playing sick, Mama will creep up on you, slide the covers down real slow like and let that extension cord come down like the Wrath of God all up and down your back and behind. That woman will have your mouth screaming and your body wailing and flailing so hard, and so fast that the Power of the Holy Beat Down zips you into that bathroom, whips you into your clothes, and flips you into the second pew of the Mount Sinai-New-Salem Zion-Baptist Church-Holy Outreach-Ministry.

Now, I remember this one particular Sunday morning when Mama greets one of the elders of the church, by the name of Mrs. Bailey. "Good morning, Mrs. Jenkins. That sure is a lovely hat you're wearing this morning."

"Oh, why thank you, Mrs. Bailey," replies Mama as she pats her hat and escorts Gloria and me up the church steps. Mama had seen that hat at the Millinery shop down on Lincoln Avenue one day last week, when we're coming from my tap dancing lesson.

It's a powdery pink, gorgeous number with a long turned down bib that loops down across Mama's face and swoops down across her shoulders in the back and it has a sheer flowing pink band that lays long and fluffy across Mama's back. Mama snatches that hat up so fast, that the sales lady has to run outside and give Mama her change.

Well anyway, on this particular Sunday, Mrs. Bailey sits in back of Mama. Now, I find that awfully peculiar, since she usually sits all the way on the other side with the rest of the Hen Network. Well, that's what I call them, because it seems like they're always a cluck-clucking and a clack-clacking about somebody's body.

Rev. Ashbury is in rare form this morning. "Hmmmmmm... Hmm...Hmmmm...Ah saida...Ah saida...When my time comes ta meet my Gawd...Hmmmah...Hmmmmah...ah wanna be a...ah wanna be a…ah saida…ah saida…ah wanna be…JUSTIFIIIIIIIED Y'ALL!"

Then the organ adds a little flavor with a DAH…DAH… DAH…DUUUUNE…DO…DO… DOONE.

All the while, Mrs. Bailey is sitting in the back of us, waving (her fan) and a rocking, rocking and waving. "Yessss Reverend, aye heah ya Reverend, preach on Reverend."

"Because ah wannabe…Aye saida…Aye saida…I wannabe…Justifiiied Y'all!" Then Rev. Ashbury starts hurling his purplish robed arms across the air and starts to vibrate like a freshly oiled motor.

(DUNE…DUNE…DUNE…DAH).

"When I stand befo' my GAWD…I wannabe…ugh," The Reverend pops and jerks his back and pops and jerks his back again, "Ahhh saida…I wannabe…Ya…Justifiiied…Ya!"

And the organ answers him with a screaming DA…DA… DA…DOW! The Reverend struts his stuff across that altar, like a rooster in a hen house and he whips out a handkerchief from nowhere and mops his face, "OWWW LAWD…OWWW LAWD!" He runs across the altar with each "Owww Lawd," and the organ works itself into a frenzy. And it screeches out a note so high and so long it can tumble down the walls of Jericho!

Out of nowhere, I hear a "WHHOOOOOOOOH!" Mrs. Bailey jumps up like a jack-in-the-box and spreads out her arms and cries, "GEE-SUS, GEE-SUS, GEE-SUSSA!" Now, I think that I should tell you, Mrs. Bailey ain't no petite woman. She weighs a good 350 lbs. if she weighs an ounce and every time she starts to praying she looks like she's crying.

Well anyway, her arms are stretched out like she's ready for the Good Lord to zoom her up on the Holy Roller rocket ship. Next thing I know, she throws back her head and starts wailing like a banshee. Her body is rolling and gyrating one way and the flab is rolling and gyrating the other way, and I guess she's dancing for the flabby ghost, because ain't NOTHING holy about this dance. Before you can say 'Jacob's Ladder' this non-stop wailing woman rips Mama's hat from her head and starts tearing it up in the name of the Holy Ghost…what did she do that for?

For a moment it seems as if Mama is in a trance. She just sits there and she doesn't say nothing or do nothing. She just watches this woman tear at her hat like a cat on a rug post. Then Mama's mouth drops south to her chest her lips start to quiver. Mama hurls her narrow behind across that pew, and she's on Mrs. Bailey, like Jesse Owens to a racetrack. Mama bum rushes that woman and slams her down to the floor and at this point all I can see is Mama's fist giving that woman's face a good work-out and all I can hear are Mrs. Bailey's muffled cries, "Ah save me Jesus, save me Lawd. Pleeez get this woman up off me."

Part II

Circa 1967

(RAT-A-TAT-TAT) "MY Grandbaby WILL be coming to see ME this summer Selma. So shut yo mouth and pack HER bags, cause that's all there is to it!"

(RAT-A-TAT-TAT) "She's MY child Mama and I'll raise her as I see fit!" Big Mama and my Mama are firing Tommy guns at each other through the courtesy of Ma Bell. Now Mama doesn't know it, but I creep into the other room and I ease the other phone off of the hook with the help of a pencil, because if Mama catches me ease-dropping on HER conversation, I'm as dead as John Dillinger!

(RAT-A-TAT-TAT) "Wait now, wait, did I hear you kerrectly, ya did say CHILE now didn't ya? Or did ya say circus animal, 'cause that's just how you treat that po' chile Selma. (Pause) Now I don't know, when the Good Lawd will see fit ta call me ta Glory, but befo' my body turns cold; I would like to see my Grandbaby…that's all."

(RAT-A-TAT-TAT) "Awwww Lawd…she done whipped out the Hattie McDaniel (first black actress to win an Oscar)."

(RAT-A-TAT-TAT) "Listen heah SELMA LOUISE JENKINS, and listen heah good! HELL will be YO playground, if you don't let me see that chile. 'Cause as long as I have breath in MY body, I REFUSE to let that chile spend THIS summer in some hot lil' cramped up room, toe tapping, and a arm flapping, like a trained monkey. So make the reservations Sugar, 'Cause I WILL be seeing MY grandbaby getting off that morning train next weekend!" Big Mama smacks that phone down, like Ali smacking down Frazier…BAM!

And I press my lips together and my hands together and I have a smirking party, behind the safety of the wallpaper. 'Cause it seems to me that Big Mama has chewed up MY Mama into bite-size, child-like pieces. I don't know about you, but I love it when my Mama is brought down to my size.

It's the summer of my 12th year, and you can bet yo bottom dollar that after all that nit-picking and niggling from Big Mama (my maternal grandmother), Mama packs my behind off to Alabama so quick, she nearly forgets my train tickets. Finally on that train, I take in a deep breath on something, something I ain't known before, something called freedom. And Mama's invisible chains burst loose and that endless shackle of lessons pops loose. And I tell you… I tell YOU…I'm riding high on this freedom train.

And I looove me some Big Mama, she's a big ole woman with an even bigger smile, a sunshine kinda smile and my favorite time of the day is when the evening is setting in. After all the chores are done and we've sat down to a gut buster of a dinner, we sit out on the porch afterwards and watch the setting sun scrape across the corn fields.

She rocks in her rocking chair and I rock beside her on the porch stair. Her hair is stone white, and she wears it in two thick plaits, one on each side, with short nappy sprigs by her forehead and there's a cigar poking out from one side of her mouth. She catches the ashes with her cupped hand. When her hand is full, she scatters the ashes to the wind. One evening I ask her why she does this, and she cocks her head and says, "Why it's for the dead and the dying Chile, for the dead and the dying."

Big Mama is a natural born story teller. She can whip up a story quicker than Bisquick can whip up a biscuit. I can always tell when the funny part is coming up, because she cracks a grin and her front gold tooth glimmers in the evening sun, and when the story reaches its final destination and the punch-line pops out at ya, Big Mama slaps her thick thighs and throws back her head and whoops, "OOOh Lawd, have mercy!" She gets tickled and then I get tickled, and I don't know which one is funnier, watching her laugh, or the story itself. Just when that pot of hot, boiling laughter is about to cool down, Big Mama rolls her eye balls this way and that way and haunches in her shoulders, and leans over, and starts tickling my already aching sides and gets that pot boiling again.

She has a real passion for the Brer Rabbit, the Sly Fox and Uncle Remus. On this particular evening I feel a bit too grown up for the familiar antics of that smart-alecky rabbit and his friends in the briar patch. I'm craving for something that's a little bit more sophisticated, something like…Mama. So I say, "Tell me a story about Mama."

"OOOh Chile, now you know yo Mama was always a bad Mamba-Jamba. Why she was always mo' woman than she ever was a chile and the biggest thing on her was always that head. Chile so tiny, look like you can roll her up and pop her in yo mouth."

"But I wanna hear a real story about Mama," I protest, pounding my fist against my thigh.

She pokes out her mouth and looks at me with suspicious eyes and says, 'Now I know that Selma done told you mo stories about her childhood, than the devil has sin."

"Ugh-ugh," I say, shaking my head. "Every time I ask her something, she starts rolling her head and puts her hand on that hip of hers, and says, let the past be the past," I say, with a mocking curl to my lips, and a bat in my eye.

Well, upon hearing this, Big Mama rest her head against the back of that chair, and starts sucking down on that cigar real hard like and says, "Hmmm, Hmmm, well, we'll just see about that." Her eyes narrow and search across that corn field like she's looking for something and she cups her hands to the sides of her mouth and shouts, "Old Man Past…Old Man Past; we're calling you out! You've been tucked away far too long. You may be hiding, but we're coming in ta get ya, me and my Annie Mae!" She cuts her eyes at me, and winks joking at me. Then she wallops out a hail of laughter and I crinkle my eyes and follow suit, and then Big Mama rolls her big eyes around again and haunches in her shoulders again, but this time I scoot away, because I know, if I don't, those hands are going to come down like thundering and lightning and give me an attack of the tickles.

Big Mama leans farther back in the chair and takes a deep pull on her cigar and circles of smoke travel above my head and beneath my nose. Big Mama is justa rocking and thinking, thinking and a rocking. I listen to the cawing of the crows that perch on the scarecrow, in the middle of the field. I watch them gnawing and plucking away at Grandpa's old derby hat and clothes. Their caws and clapping wings tear through the seams of silence.

"Well," she finally says, staring at the crows circling the sky. "Ta tell ya the truth, we was so po that yo mama didn't have too much time for book learning, but she got plenty of Mother wit, and sometimes that mother wit can take you farther than all of the book learning in the world. Lawd, she could fight, that chile took ta fighting quicker than a fish ta water."

"Why, I remember this one time the Willie Parson's Boys, naw, naw, wait now, the Willie McClain boys, that's right, the Willie McClain Boys, keep on bothering yo mama and the rest of my chi'ren every day at school. Now, ya see, they thought they were sid ditty (Grand) because their father was the undertaker for all of the black folks in the county at that time. So naturally, they always had decent shoes and decent clothes ta wear ta school everyday. Selma and the rest of my chi'ren are just as raggedy as a Hebrew Slave and not one pair of shoes between 'em. "

"Well anyway, like I was saying, every morning the McClain Boys will catch 'em and whip their asses from rip rump ta appetite. They'll say, "There goes the Ellisons, let's get 'em, let's get 'em." Those boys will finish ripping off their already raggedy ass clothes."

"Well, on this particular morning, Selma gets up way befo anybody else in the house. She announces that she'll be the only one attending school this morning. And I ask her why and she looks at me all strange like and says, 'got business to tend to,' and she leaves it at that and I don't really remembers why, but I leaves it at that too."

"Now she's only 10 at the time and the chile so skinny, she can use a wet noodle as a sliding board. Sure enough, half way down the road who does she meet up with…?" and she points her finger at me, and I shout out, "The McClain Boys!"

"Hmmm, Hmmm, that's right," she says, steadily rocking and smoking. "Sure enough, they're ready ta git down wit the git down. Yo Mama whips out a brick from her satchel with break neck speed and commences to whip their nat'ral bone asses with that very brick and Baby I tell YOU it's time for those chi'ren ta give their tails ta Selma and their souls ta God. She beats three of em down ta the ground and the other two take off running, screaming and yelping like scared pigs."

"Later on, after they have called me ta school and the big issue is all over with, I ask yo mama was she scared of tackling those big bull babies (a male child). She cocks her head and thinks about it for a second and says, "How can I be afraid of something I can't see?" Then I ask her was she fighting wit her eyes close. And she says, "Naw Mama, my eyes are wide open, but the only thing I can see in front of me is a curtain…a curtain of blood."

"A curtain of blood," I ask.

"Hmmm, Hmmm, that's right chile," says Big Mama, steadily rocking and puffing on that cigar and gazing into the now dark sky.

After a high wall of silence has been built up between Big Mama and me, she hauls off and knocks it down, when she says," And that reminds me of the time waaay back in 1946,naw,naw,wait now, let me get my thoughts together, hmmmm, it was 1947. That's right 1947. Yo mama is 16 years old at the time. And Old Man Cotton is still king down in these heah parts. Now, yo mama when the spirit hits her can pick mo cotton, than Adam and Eve can make babies. Baby, when yo mama's nimble fingers start ta flicking and picking on that cotton, you'd swear up and down it was magic in her hands and you know, picking cotton is painful thing and it'll make yo fingers bleed and sting to da bone, but yo Mama never paid it no mind. It's like she's in a trance or somptin."

"Baby, she'll pile that cotton up so high, it looks like snow in July."

"Now, on this particular evening, I'm mid-wifing over in Dothan County and I ain't due back till that following day. So the story I'm about ta tell ya, I've been able to piece it together from what I've seen myself, from Selma, friends and family."

"Now, where was I? Oh yes, that's right. On this particular evening, it took four men with strong backs ta haul yo mama's cotton up on that scale and at this time the going rate for picking cotton is ten dollars for every hundred pounds. Now, Mr. Henry, the owner of the mill, when he sees all this cotton, his mind musta start clicking like a Timex. Now you see,this white man ain't really no white man, he's a pink man. Chile, that man's skin is just a pink and greasy looking. He looks like a giant blister, that's just about ta bust."

"And he says, "Oh Lawdy, Lawdy. Look-a-heah, look-a-heah," and he takes his handkerchief and dabs it across his face and all across his neck. He always wears the same straw hat with a black band on it and you can just tell that it's too tight for his big head, cause the rest of his face is ballooning out on the sides and he's got a big ole' fat gut that flops over his belt buckle. Then he says, "OOOH wee, if that lil'gal can't pick cotton, eggs ain't poultry, grits ain't grocery and Mona Lisa was a man!" Come on now boys, bring that load right over heah, right over heah," he says pointing at the scale."

"What kinda scale is it Big Mama," I ask. "Is it the kinda scale that you weigh fruit on in the grocery store?"

"Oooh no Baby, it's much bigger than that, it's kinda like the scale that people weigh on, 'cept that the numbers go up waay high and it has a wider base at the bottom."

"So, he snatches his pen and notebook out of his shirt pocket and he licks his pen one good time and says, "Let's see what we got heah," and every time he talks his jowls shake like a bowl of soup."

"So, Mr. Henry has all of the sacks of cotton loaded on top of each other on this scale and he's resting one hand on the top of the scale. The scale is justa creaking and a bouncing, bouncing and a creaking and all eyes are stuck to that long, bouncing red needle, like hair to a drain pipe. That slick, no count Mr. Henry knows this, ya see? So that long red needle is a dropping and a bobbing and it hits 1300 lbs and with a slight motion of his hand on the back of the scale he shifts the weight gage. That long red needle jumps down to 800 lbs and he slides his hand back up to the top of the scale."

"Now, you know and I know, that yo mama don't miss a beat. She sees what that man just did. Some of the other workers see it too, but the difference between her and them is that she ain't afraid of standing up for her rights. Now Baby, believe me it was a hell of a thang to see, this little 16 year ole black chile approaching that big white man and remembers Baby, these were dangerous, treacherous times for a person of color." Mama says, with squinting eyes.

"Selma twists her mouth and puts one hand on her hip and points at the scale with the other. And that chile says, "You got yo fools mixed up Mr. Henry. 'Cause we both know that scale read 1300 lbs!""

"Now, everybody knows about this wad of rolled up money that Mr. Henry carries around in his side pocket. Honey, that thang is about the size of a baseball. To tell you the truth everybody wonders why that damn thang never slips out. Well, he looks at her kinda under eyed-like and sort of smiles at Selma and digs into his side pocket and pulls out that big bankroll and he licks his thumb and index finger and peels that chile off 80 dollars. And he says, "Why Gal ya know I can't give ya, what I don't owe ya." "

"And Selma continues to stand there with that one hand on her hip and justa stomping her feet, and looks that man dead in his eyes and says, "What you owe me Mr. Henry, is 130 dollars." Mr. Henry cuts his eyes at the rest of the workers and says in a real low voice, "Ya making a scene Gal, now you gone and take this money or get the hell outta my face." Well, seeing how we need the money and all, yo mama gulps down her lump of pride and snatches up the money and slits her eyes at that man."

"Now it was yo Grandpa's job ta look after the chi'ren that evening since he knows I'm mid-wifing and all, but the only thing yo Grandpa was looking after that evening was a gin bottle. He gets pissy drunk that night and passes out like a dead man. Now, Selma has always been a firm believer in the saying that opportunity is like a bald head man."

"But why is it like a bald head man, Big Mama," I ask.

"Because it's a slippery thang Baby, so when ya get holds ta it, better hold on tight. Now, where was I, hmmm, oh yes, that's right, yo mama creeps into Grandpa's room and steals his gun that he keeps at his bedside."

"Because when Old Man Trouble comes ta blowing through the front door, he gone take that gun and blow him straight out the backdoor! Now, as I was saying, that chile walks 15 miles for justice that night with that gun in her hand."

"Do you think she means to kill Mr. Henry, Big Mama?"

"Ta tell you the truth, I don't think she does but I do believe she means ta scare the Be-Jesus outta him. Now, for all intents and purposes, she can take the truck, but with that noisy, clunky old thang he can probably hear her a mile away."

"So yo mama sets about walking those 15 miles and from the way I hear it, she meets several friends on the road that night. When they go ta greet her or offer her a ride, she doesn't open her mouth. She just looks straight ahead and seeps into the darkness with that gun glinting in the moonlight.

"It takes her nearly half the night ta makes it to Mr. Henry's place and when she gets there, it's lit up like a Christmas tree. At first she thinks that the man is having a party or sumptin, but she doesn't hear any noises coming from inside the house."

"So Selma creeps around ta the back way and peeks into Mr. Henry's bedroom window and there he is as big as life snoring like a damn grizzly bear, with every blasted light on in the house. I guess that man done did so much wrong doing, he's afraid the haints (ghosts) will get him in the dark."

Selma slides through that window just as easy as hot butter. She tips over ta the side of that man's bed and cocks that gun into his temple and says, "Wake up Motha Fucka, fo I blow yo brains out." And ole man Mr. Henry jumps up like a dog to a bone!"

"What happens then Big Mama, what happens then?"

"Wait Baby, wait, Big Mama's gonna tell ya, shhh, now where was I? Hmmm, oh yes, that's right," she says, popping her finger.

"Whaaaa, whaaa, what's going on? How the hell did you git in heah?" he says. Then he realizes that it's a sawed-off gun fitted dead at in his head. And his eyes start popping out, like a bullfrog's. And then Selma says, 'It's time ta piss or get off the pot ole man, now give me MY money," she shouts, with her finger still on that trigger.

"Okay, okay, lil gal, don't get too hasty now, don't get too hasty," he says, slowly, pulling his pants off a nearby chair.

"And befo you can say Jack Diddley Daniels that fool takes those pants and smacks Selma dead in the face with the belt buckle. And Selma gets scared and starts showering down bullets like manna from heaven. And Mr. Henry's money swirls across that room like a witch on a broomstick. And that gun in her hand is as hot as a fire cracker, so she throws it down and swoops up fifty dollars off of the floor, and jets over to the window. That girl straddles that window sill and she has one foot on the road ta freedom when she feels something jerking and twisting at her ankle. Mr. Henry has that chile's ankle in a death grip and refuses ta let go. And he yanks and pulls on her leg so hard until he yanks her down on top of him. And then they get ta tussling and wallowing in a pool of blood. She wrestles with that man, likes she's wrestling with the devil. And every time that chile tries ta get up, his blood and his hands plops her right back down."

"And every thang gets real quiet and he ain't fighting her no mo. He ain't doing nothing no mo. And his eyes are looking far, far away. She watches his breath barely rising and falling from his chest. And this time she doesn't even bother ta stand up. She crawls over to a dry spot and then she stands up and finally keeps her balance. Then she looks down at her hands and they've been bathed in blood, his blood. And she tries to wipe them off on her dress, but it's sopped in blood too, his blood. And that chile stares at her hands and she screams and screams. She can't stop screaming. And she tries ta wipe her hands in her hair, but it's soaked in blood too, his blood. And she finally decides to walk with her backside scraping against the wall over towards the window, trying her best not to step in that blood. And she steps over Mr. Henry's body, and he lifts his head up one last time and he slowly raises his hand as if it weighs a hundred pounds and he points at her. And a popping sound is forming in that man's chest, it sounds like a pot brought to a high boil. And his mouth forms a perfect O and he moans, "you…youuuuu," and he collapses on the floor like a sack of bones. And Selma tears outta that window justa screaming and a hollering to the top of her lungs. And she runs down that road like she's being chased by hell hounds. And every now and then she looks back, making sure he ain't gonna run out and grab her."

"It's nearly sun up now, and Selma has the good sense to hide out in the woods until night fall. And when I arrive home that morning, who do I see making himself at home in MY house? None other than that low-down, good for nothing sheriff, he has his feet all propped up on MY furniture, and justa puffing and a sucking on his pipe. And yo Granddaddy is seating across the room staring him down. And I can tell that yo Granddaddy is feeling mighty froggish. He's about ready ta jump that sheriff and drive a two by fo' up his natra ass! It's probably a good thang that Selma did take that gun, 'cause me and yo Granddaddy would have taking turns pumping holes in that ass."

"And after a whole bunch of small talk, he gets around ta asking me, what he really came there ta ask me. And natrally, I tells him that I ain't seen Selma, which I hadn't. So he goes about the business of packing his pipe, and lightening it back up. And his lips are a working and a wrapping around that pipe like a fish's mouth, trying his best to keep that thang lit. "Well, that's alright," he says, shaking his match out, "She'll show up sooner or later…her kind always does." "

"And sure enough come nightfall that chile bust through that door like a wind storm. And she runs up ta me, screaming and a wailing, "I killed em Mama, I killed 'em…I done killed that man!" And then she runs ta this wall and that wall, and just about every wall in the house saying, "I killed 'em Mama…I killed 'em!" And all that blood has dried up and caked up on that chile like Georgia clay, and this sweet. sickly odor is pushing up off her body. And I try ta grab hold ta the chile and tell her that Mr. Henry isn't dead at all, that he has lost a lot of blood, but he ain't dead. And she looks at me with far away eyes, and she cups her mouth, and she laughs this foolish kinda laugh. And she rolls around on the floor and her legs start ta spinning like a Ferris wheel. And she shoots up like bullet and starts ta swatting flies that aren't even there."

"Well, I do everything I can do for her that night. I bath her and change her clothes, but it's awfully hard on the chile, we have ta keep her quiet and hide her in a musty ole foot locker on and off for two days, until we can make arrangements ta have her moved up to Chicago with my sister."

"And just as sure as I'm black, that mean ole sheriff comes prowling around, and sneaking around my house again. He's mad now, justa huffin' and a puffin' like a steam engine. And Chile' he ram sacks my house from top ta bottom, he searches my house, like he's searching for tomorrow! That man has torn up my house three times looking for Selma. And the last time he's madder than a bulldog with rabies.

"And Baby, in my heart of hearts I know two wrongs ain't never made a right. And what that chile did was wrong…wrong…wrong, shooting that man like that! I also know, that if the Good Lawd had seen fit for my chile to walk outta that jail cell alive…a part of her would have been sprawled out dead, on that jail house flo'. And I know this Chile, just as sure as I know, that the sun will shine. Because down heah Baby, justice for a black man, ain't no justice at all and they don't take kindly ta no black man or let alone a black woman harming nobody white!" And Big Mama's voice swells up with emotion and I reach up and take hold of her hand. She looks down and gives me a weak smile and squeezes my hand a bit and sort of rubs my fingers. She tightens her eyes and takes in a deep breath.

I hurry up and say, "So Mama makes it to the north okay, huh Big Mama?"

"Yes Baby she sho do. That ole sheriff thinks he's slick, but hmmmp, we sho him he needs a lil' bit mo greasing. He sets up road blocks from heah to Tennessee, but we outsmart that ole possum!"

"We dress yo mama up as a lil boy and stuff her hair under a bib cap and get her on board that Greyhound Bus. And yo Granddaddy, God bless his soul, travels with her. And we change his appearance around too. We give him a long beard and put some blackberry juice on his face ta make his skin color darker. 'Cause we just know that if that sheriff stops that bus he'll recognize him as quick as he would a dollar bill. And do you know that slick sheriff has that bus stopped… twice?"

"And I was soooo grateful that when the Lawd saw fit for the chile ta travel, that her mind was half way fit too. At first, I wasn't sure which was worst, my baby losing her mind like that or if she would have spent a night in that white man's jail cell. And at the time it liked ta (almost) have killed me," she says snapping her finger.

"But Baby, looking back on it now, I think maybe, that was God's way, God's way of punishing us both for awhile. But in the end

He fixed it…Ahh yes, He fixed it," Big Mama says, biting down on her lower lip and rocking in her chair.

Then Big Mama stares up at the sky like she's sending up a silent prayer. And I can swear that I see Big Mama sneak in a tear and she palms it away on the sly. She scatters ashes to the wind for the last time that evening, and she wipes her hands together. Then she gives them a hard push down the sides of her dress, as if she's trying to push away the past.

Two years later Big Mama is diagnosed with sugar diabetes and she has her left leg amputated. After that I think Big Mama gets mad at the pure-dee world and sort of gives up on life. So she closes her eyes one day and goes into a diabetic coma and she never reopens them again. Sometimes, late at night, if I lay my head real still on my pillow and shut my eyes, I can see Big Mama's face smiling down on me.

I just know that if there is a heaven above that Big Mama is somewhere up there, perched on her little cloud stool, surrounded by baby angels with fat cheeks and fluttering wings. They're listening to Big Mama string together her tales about *Br'er Rabbit, The Sly Fox and Uncle Remus.*

Part III

Now, before we go any farther, I think that I should tell you that in the fall of that same year, I make an important discovery. Something that Mama has tried her best to keep me away from. Something that was about to change my whole life…its music. That's right music. Now, I know about Chopin, Bach, Gershwin and all that other high-faluting stuff, but that low-down, funk-down beat? I know as much about that as a dog knows about Sunday school. I snatch glimpses of it from blaring cars or on my way home from school; I hear it sizzling out of Fat Papa's Rib Joint. I guess Fat Papa figured if the smell of sizzling rib tips wouldn't lure them in, Aretha sizzling out her funk will get the job done.

Sometimes, on Saturday mornings I will try to sneak a peek at *American Bandstand*, but it's like Mama has music radar or something. She busts up in my room like Elliot Ness and gives me those squinty eyes and turns that channel right back to *PBS,* throws her head up in the air and makes a grand exit.

The way it all comes about is on the playground, at school, at recess one day. I'm watching the other girls play. Because that's what I usually do. They don't usually play with me on account they think I'm some sort of blighte girl (want to be white) or something. The white girls obviously think the same thing too, 'cause they won't play with me either. Mama says it's because they're all jealous of my talent, and 'cause I lead the Star Spangled Banner and perform at all of the assemblies, but I think Mama's wrong. Maybe they think I'm stuck up or something and if they would just give me a slither of a chance, maybe they would see that I'm an alright person.

So, anyway, like I was saying it's a late fall day and the kids are playing and carrying on extra hard to keep that almighty hawk (the Chicago wind) from nipping and biting at their behinds, I'm walking around, jumping around trying to keep myself warm too, and

I turn to the side of the building and I see these three girls from my sixth grade class dancing and a prancing. There are two girls in the back and one girl in the front. Theresa the girl in the front has a look in her eye that's something fierce and sister's working that wind for filth! It's like she's defying that very wind. The wind is blowing in her face, tussling at her hair, and justa flapping at her coat. She waves her hands through the air, and the girls in the back wave their hands through the air and she see-saws her hips, and they see-saw their hips. She shimmies to the ground, and they shimmy to the ground and she rocks her head and opens her mouth and sings, *"My world is empty without you Babe."* The two girls in the back are stilling dancing and their doing all of this to an invisible beat. So I go up to Theresa, and say, "Hey, what y'all doing?"

Well, she stops cold dead on an attitude and cocks her head and looks at me like I have lost my frigging mind. She puts her hands on her hips and smacks her tongue and says, "What you think we're doing?"

"I don't know," I say, shrugging my shoulders. "That's why I'm asking."

She rolls her eyes, snaps her finger and says. "Miss woman puleeze, on what rocket ship did you make your crash landing? The Supremes Miss Woman, okay? The Suuuuu-premmmes! Didn't you see them on the *Ed Sullivan Show* last night?" Slowly, I shake my head. "Girrrl. puleeze, they turned that motha out," she says, while snapping in Z formation! She cocks her head and adds, "Ain't you hip at all to what's going down?" I nod my head and as I walk away I hear a thread of laughter floating against my back. I try to tell myself that it doesn't matter, but deep inside the need to fit in was like an open wound, a wound never tended to, a wound that refuse to heal.

The Supremes...The Supremes, for the rest of that afternoon, I roll that name around in my head like flour dough. The Supremes...The Supremes, after school I make a mad dash to the telephone. I tell Mama that I have to skip my voice lesson that evening due to a big test at school the following day. "I just gotta get my behind to the library and study Mama, I just gotta!" Well, naturally she protests a little bit, but eventually she gives in.

You know, thinking back on it now, the library not only houses a bunch of books, but it houses a bunch of lies too. I bet you anybody and some of everybody has at one time or another told a lie on the library. It's like that little card not only allows us to borrow books every now and then, but a few lies too. Maybe that's why they call it the lie-brary.

Well, I go to the library that afternoon alright, but it sure isn't to study any books. I step up in there to study some greasy, fat-back, neck bone, finger lickin' soul. And I stack up albums in my arms like flap-jacks on a fat man's plate. And when I sit in that booth and place those ear-phones to my head, and…LAWD have mercy, it's like BLAM! Someone's just slapped me with a brick!

My studies have taught me that Aretha Franklin's pain has been melted down and pressed into the grooves of the vinyl record. My studies have taught me that you can walk into any record shop and buy a piece of her pain for 59 cents. My studies have taught me that when Ms Aretha moans…oh when she moans, that she has somehow or another yanked her pain out of her body and slapped it upon a pedestal for all the world to see and there in that booth, I am ready to testify. I am ready to bear witness to her persecution. I whisper, "Sing your pain Miss Aretha! Sing your pain!"

That evening, when I put my key through that door, music is definitely on the menu! Mama can keep me away from friends, claiming they're not the right class of people. Mama can keep me shackled down to my lessons, claiming it's for my future, but she cannot and will not keep me away from MY music. I will guard my treasure, like a snake guards her eggs.

I devise ways of watching The Temptations on T.V. while listening to a contralto on the radio. I devise ways of watching an opera on T.V. while listening to The Marvelettes on the radio and I make sure that the door to my room is as tight as a chastity belt. The music of her choice is always pumped up the loudest while my music is low and rocking and socking. My legs are movin' and groovin' to this new found beat.

I discover this Dee Jay too, by the name of Herb Kent, the Cool Gent. His voice is as warm and comforting as a blanket and he turn tables all the new jams. He's a wizard of madness too, telling bust yo side stories about the *Gym Shoe Creeper* and the *WHA-WHO Man*. Sometimes, that fool has me whooping so hard, I have to smother my laughter into a pillow, and then if he really gets the madness percolating, I start to guffawing myself into a coughing fit and I'm rolling around in a bed of laughter, justa coughing, spitting and a praying that Mama doesn't bust me and my door wide open.

Eventually, as sure as ice makes water, Mama passes by my door and says, “Baby, I’m sure glad you’re enjoying your music so much, but can you turn it down a little?”

“Alright, Mama,” I reply, as sweet as apple butter and I jack that sucker up two more notches.

At night I tuck the transistor radio between my ear and the pillow. And I let The Temptations croon me to sleep. David Ruffin the lead singer is singing the praises of his girl. And later on in another song after that same girl has slammed him and dumped him, that poor man is hurting so bad, he just wishes it would rain!

Now, Selma Louise Jenkins ain’t no fool and she ain’t raising one either. So every morning before I leave for school, I make sure that the transistor dial is right smack on that classical dial. Just in case she gets curious and her nose starts to drooping and snooping.

Still, I wonder why she would try to deny me this music. She doesn’t deny Gloria, and she sure doesn’t deny herself, so why me? I remember Sunday evenings after dinner, Arthur stops by. Gloria and him laugh, and giggle their way into the living room and set the hi-fi ablaze and they would sure enough let their legs shake and their booties quake and they do this wild dance called the horse and they gallop that bad boy all the way home, riding the beat Booker T. and the M.G.’s!

When a mood of silence falls across the house and all of the housework is done, Mama trades in her motherhood for a telephone cord and a one-way ticket on the gossip train, to find out who say, what say, when say, and how say (and a steady stream of “Naaawwww Girl” cackles from her throat), I know what time it is. It’s time for Arthur and Gloria to get their love on and I ease myself into the back of the couch with just one eye poking out. And I get real comfortable like, so I can get my sneak on.

Suddenly, their music mood changes and the degree of light changes too. They no longer require that red, heart thumping, pumping beat. They require a blue, hip grinding, lip binding beat. At first it’s a crackling sound on the hi-fi and then The Delfonics velvetizes, *“La, La, La, means I love yooou.”* She looks into his eyes and he looks into her eyes and the music welds their hips together, their mouths together and their bodies sway together, like two leaves falling from a tree.

I remember Mama and Daddy one Christmas Eve night; I think I was about 4 years old at the time. And I creep into the living room, looking for Santa Clause. Instead I find something else all together. I find Mama and Daddy in a lustful fog. Mama's hand is draped across Daddy's shoulder, holding a glass of egg nog and her head lies upon his other shoulder. He holds her by her waist with one hand and with his free hand, he sips his whiskey. He smiles down at her with booze in his eyes and a little something on his mind. Their hips are entwined and they're doing the sho-nuf slow grind and the living room is decked out with Christmas lights. The hi-fi is wheezing out the blues *"Merry Christmas Baby, you sure did treat me nice. You bought me a diamond ring for Christmas, now I'm living in paradise."* After that Christmas the blues packed its bags and walked out the door and took Daddy with him.

And ooh, this one Saturday evening; is to be my groove evening. Mama has gone to the A&P grocery store and Gloria has gone to see a Sidney Poitier movie with Arthur, see? I dump a pile of 45's on the hi-fi and I blast those speakers like nobody's business.

I commence to do my sin. I'm as happy as a sissy in a bath house. Now, I've got the Supremes on the turn-table and I'm going at it just the way they did on Shin-Dig last night. I'm ready to turn the joint out! No, I'm not pretending to be Flo, with her drama and too much trauma self. No, I'm not pretending to be Mary, with her wannabe but can't be self. I am Miss Diana Ross, the only Diva herself. My body is shaking and even the toilet tissue in my training bra is quaking. I'm jerking and a working to that *Motown* Beat. *"Love is like a itching in my heart, tearing all apart and Baby, I can't scratch it,"* and ...GRRRRREWWWW!

I hear this scratch that tears at my 45 and it seems to ripple across the floor and tears the skin off my back, exposing bone and shredded meat! I jump and turn around and it's Mama! It's always Mama, when I sleep its Mama, when I breathe its Mama, when I pee its Mama. Mama gets slits for eyes, dangerous eyes, cut through me like a bullwhip eyes.

She snatches off The Supremes and snaps that record in half and she waves and fans the pieces in my face. She hauls off and smacks me in my face. She smacks me in my face so hard, for a second I can't see nothing but a gazillion stars and for what...listening to music...music?

"You've been sneaking around listening ta this shit! What the fuck else you been sneaking around doing behind my back huh...huh," she steps closer and closer and her breath is on me like a wild dog's.

"Nothing," I scream to the top of my lungs, "NOTHING!" I run and slide down into the nearest corner and shield my face with my arms.

"I work hard; I scrimp and save every damn cent ta give you lessons. I do everything short of selling my ass ta give you a chance at a better life and this is how you repay me, by listening to this damn jigger boo shit? Is it? …Is it?" She leans over me with her right hand stretched out, ready to slap me into next Tuesday.

"Please Mama, please," I scream. "Don't hit me no more, please!" I try to wrap myself into a tight little ball, wishing I can just roll away. Mama stands over me with a teaspoon of mercy and she takes a deep breath and steps backward. My lips feel like they've been shot full of Novocain. The bottom one is ballooning and blood is trickling from the side.

This is what they expect outta us, Annie Mae," she says, waving the broken record. "All of this shoo-bop-de-bop bull shit. We've been singing this shit ever since we got off the damn boat, and it still ain't got us a pot ta piss in," then she looks at me with concern in her eyes. "I want something better for you Annie Mae, something much better."

I glue my courage together and I yell, "You listen to it, Gloria listens to it? So why can't I listen to it?"

"Because I want you to be special, goddammit, more than this bull shit," she says, hurling the pieces to the floor.

"I don't want to be special…I want to be me," I scream. "Me," I say, blowing snot to the roof of my nose and pounding my hand on my chest. Slowly, she bends over me and my heart is thumping out of my chest and I just know that I'm going to pay for my loose tongue. I want to run, but she has me cornered.

Instead, she smoothes the hair out of my face and says, "Baby, it's only a handful of black opera singers and Baby, I know, as sure as I know that my eyes are black, that you can be one of them. You see Baby, when you open your mouth and that aria spills out, you're waaay over in White Man's land and they don't know how ta deal with that. It makes them mighty uncomfortable and that's when YOU demand THEIR respect and they've gots to give you yo propers! Baby, I want that for you so bad, so bad, I can taste it, but you've gotta want it for yourself Annie Mae," she says still massaging my face. Now tell me, what you want? What do you want for yourself?"

I suck in a deep breath of courage and I say, "I want you to leave me alone," and I scoot out from under her and dart towards the hi-fi. "Because of you, I don't have any friends at school. Because of you, they think I'm some kinda freak. Because of you…you…YOU," and after each you I stomp my feet on the floor so hard, it reads on the Richter scale. "Why don't you just lock me away…huh ? Just lock me away and forget about ME!"

That's when I notice one of Mama's most priced possessions, in all of its shining glory. It sits on a small table, on the side of the hi-fi. It's a yellow crystal phoenix. Daddy won it for Mama at *Riverview* one summer (there's a label on the bottom that reads made in Japan). The base looks like orange tongues of fire bursting upward and the eyes look like fiery red stones and when the sunlight hits it just so, it looks like a burning yellow flame. Sometimes, when me and Gloria will be cleaning and dusting in the front room, Mama will holler out, "Don't y'all break my phoenix up in there! Or I'll break my foot up y'all asses!" Now I cut my eyes at her…and I cut my eyes at the phoenix…I cut my eyes at her…and BOOM! I knock that sucker to the floor and haul my behind out of that house as if it's on fire!

I'm running and running and I can't stop running and I'm afraid to stop running, because if I do I'll feel the crack of Mama's belt on my behind. My lungs feel tight and tingly, and I catch hold of a street lamp and my breath. I look up and darkness has melted across the sky And although, it's a fall chill in the air, my face is as hot as a grill. I see the floating head lights of cars passing by and I make up my mind that night that I'm going someplace, into the arms of a man.

Now you see at that time, during the 60's and 70's and before the yuppie invasion of the 80's, Halsted and Willow is a multi-racial neighborhood, there are Blacks, Hispanics, Italians and Yugoslavians. It's a blue collar neighborhood filled with blue collar dreams. We lived in peace, racial harmony and the pursuit of a larger paycheck.

Now, I just know where I can find my father on a Saturday night, or just about any night, at the almighty Barrel House. Now you see, at this time the Barrel House sits on the corner of Halsted and North Avenue (now on this very spot sits a respectable bank). If you pass by the Barrel House at any given time, you might see just about any thing. You might see, women waving knives, because that's her man, and don't know-bodies bodies mess with HER man. You might see pimps beating their investments down, because they came up short on the nightly total. You might see a man beating down a woman, who he thought was a woman, but turned out to be a lot of a man. You know that kinda thing.

But if you ask me, this place is a temple, where the drunks, thugs, wine heads and the rest of the street wranglers come to worship their god…the drink…the almighty drink, that drink that can make you wanna slap your own Mama! I'm talking about that drink that can make you do the hoochie coochie dance butt naked in front of Mother Theresa. I'm talking about that drink that can make you wake up in the morning next to a gorilla in your bed, and you wonder, what the hellll…..! Now, that's the kinda drink that I'm talking about!

Now in the back of the Barrel House are the El Tracks, and underneath you're sure to find some members of the congregation gathering here and there. Its so many broken whiskey bottles and wine bottles back there, until it looks like scattered fairy dust shining in the moon light.

To the left of me I see a female worshipper standing in the shadows, letting go of her pee and her pride. She has less than a handful of mangy grey hair on her head. Now her hair isn't long enough for a rubber band and yet she figures she should adorn it with a filthy ribbon that's plastered on the side. I guess it's a token of better days and her face has seen better days too (looks like the footprints of time has used her face for a Mexican hat dance). Do you know she has the gall to smile at me, while she's pulling up her panties? Well, I try to smile back, but I sure don't feel too comfortable about it.

A few feet away, I spot another member of the congregation stretched out on the ground, on the side of the building as if he's lounging at the *Ritz Carlton* There's a raggedy coat snatched up to his neck and a wine bottle snatched up to his head. He looks up at me with a toothless grin and black leather skin and says, "Gal, hey Gal, what yo ass doing out heah this time of night? Ya better get yo ass home, 'fo one of these freakaphiles get hold of yo young ass."

I stare down at him and ask, "You seen my daddy?"

"What's yo daddy's name Gal? I can't help ya if you don't tell me his name. Shiiit, it's a whole lotta fathers up in there. And a whole lotta Motha Fuckas too…KE…KE…KE…KE," he says, laughing at his own joke and bringing the bottle back up to his head.

"William, William Jenkins," I answer and I realize how cold I am and that even this drunk has sense enough to have a coat on, even if it is a Goodwill reject. I rub my arms with my hands.

"Awww, ya talking about Skillet, Skillet Jenkins. Yeah, he's got his black ass up in there, check all the way to the back."

Two of the worshippers rush pass me and they're laughing so hard, until one of them has to rest against the hood of a car. The other one fans out a deck of 20 Dollar Bills. "Girl, did you see 'em? Did you see that big ass fool Girl?" The one against the car is laughing so hard she's sliding down.

"Girrrrl, I milked that Motha Fucka, like I was milking a pregnant Jersey cow, do you hear me?"

"And that Motha Fucka was so drunk he'd kiss an orangutan's ass and call it Mama," the other one says, clutching her money and her stomach at the same time.

"You ain't no good girl. You heah me? You ain't no damn good at all," says the other one, while balling up her money and stuffing it into her bra.

When I open up the doors, two things slap me in the face, the stench of beer and the thunder of voices. The bar is a big wooden circle that's hallowed out in the middle. And the two bartenders that work the bar are really the high priests and they do the bidding of the beer guzzling worshippers who have come to give praise. The bartenders are working so fast and so hard, diamonds of sweat pop off their foreheads, like popcorn in a skillet and they're pouring, rubbing, wiping and slapping the almighty sacrament down. Most of the congregation consists of tricks and their treats (women who turn tricks) and as I pass by some of the treats, it becomes mighty obvious to me that most of them have chosen to bathe themselves in "Jean Nate" instead of soap and water. "Hey, what is she doing in here," one of the treats yells out.

"Hey girl, get yo ass up outta heah," one of the drunks mumbles, as he slobbers into his drink. I pay him no mind; I head straight for the back room to find my Daddy.

In the backroom there are worshippers too, but they're not there to worship the drink as much as they're worshipping another god and goddess, the almighty dollar and Lady Luck.

I swing open the back door and I see a red cloth spread out in the middle of the floor surrounded by kneeling men, stacks of money and cubes of dice on the side. One of the kneeling men grabs hold of the dice and lifts them up towards his lips and starts to praying and whispering into the dice. He has scissor like teeth and tiny welts for eyes. You know how a robber looks when he's wearing a stocking cap over his face so he won't be recognized? Well, that's how this man looks, except for those frigging teeth that stand out like a sore thumb. Now,I maybe wrong as two left shoes, but it sure seems to me, that instead of having 32 molars in his head, this man has a good 64. They are so sharp, and so jagged that he can probably give a shark some fierce competition "Ahhh,I got it on the run now," he says as he shakes the dice. "Take me home sweet mama, take yo sweet lovin' Daddy home!" Then he swings the dice across the cloth, and calls out "Ha…Ha…Haaagh!" And he opens his mouth and he flashes that man-eating grin and all you can see are white teeth stretching from here to the Great Wall of China. He bends over and collects his money.

There's a pretty white woman standing in the corner near my daddy, with a waist cinching, hip clinching, red velvet dress on with short, blonde, bouncing curls and cool blue eyes. I can't help but to wonder does she use those blue eyes to get my daddy drunk, drunk enough to pay her rent. She has her elbow propped up on his shoulder. He's sipping on his drink and looking down at her boobs as if they're a national monument.

"Daddy," I yell.

Mo' Teeth looks at me and then at my father and gnashes his teeth together and says, "Hey, Skillet, get this kid outta here. She ain't got no business up in here!" The other kneeling worshippers let out a few impatient groans and a few ahh shits are sprinkled here and there.

He walks towards me with hurried steps, a tight lip, and a sucked in jaw. "Annie Mae, what the hell you doing here," he ask. He narrows his eyes and adds, "Did Selma send you down here?"

And slowly, I shake my head, as he escorts me outside. "Then what the hell are you doing down here, with no coat on? What's wrong with you?" And I can tell that this man has about as much time and patience for me as a pig has for table manners.

And I open my mouth to talk, but nothing comes out. My breath gets short and I start heaving like an accordion and my tears and snot mingle together and start running down the side of my mouth. I can feel my face getting hot and starting to burn again and I want to control myself in front of Daddy, but I can't…I just can't. It's as if just the sight of this man has turned me into an emotional avalanche, an avalanche that just falls, crumbles and rolls unto the concrete.

"What's wrong with you Annie Mae?" And I see his chest now, rising and falling under his jacket and I just KNOW if I can find my way to his chest, that I'll find my way home. As if sensing what

I'm planning on doing, that man takes his hands and holds me at bay. He grabs my arms so tight until the blood underneath refuses to circulate.

I'm shaking my head…I'm shaking my head in disbelief, that my own Daddy won't let me hold him. I can't understand why! And I'm looking up at him, and he's looking down at me, with eyes that are cold, cold…killer eyes…stone eyes…I don't give a damn eyes!

But you see, I don't care how he looks at me. I intend to hold this man, and that's just what I am going to do. My hands are swimming now, swimming in the air, swimming for his chest, trying to find my way home.

"Go home, Annie Mae," he says with a deep sigh, "just go on home," his patience is as thin as wet tissue paper.

"I'm not going home without you, Daddy. I ain't EVER going back there without you!"

And still, that man refuses to let me hold him. I can't help but to wonder, what's wrong, is it me? Why can't I hold MY daddy…why? "Daddy, please come home again and make it like it was before. Mama's driving me crazy. She won't let me do nothing, but take those stupid lessons. Please come home, Daddy, please!" I see that I'm getting nowhere, so with a deep sigh of release, I step back and I stare him dead in those killer eyes and I see it then it's been there all of the time, right there in his pupils and it hits me like a black jack a black jack to my forehead. I take another step back and I say, "You blame me for all of the problems between you and Mama, don't you?" I place my hand on my chest and again I say, "You blame me for all of the problems between you and Mama?"

He looks down at his shoes and slides them across the pavement (making an invisible line between us) and shoves his hands deep into his pockets and says, "Go home, Annie Mae…just go home." Opportunity has left itself wide open and I leap to his chest. He eases his hands from his pockets and raises them high above his head and I have finally found my way home. But wasn't it Thomas Wolfe that said, you can never go home again? Well, Mr. Wolfe was right. Because I can feel tenseness in Daddy's chest that says, I'm not wanted there. A tenseness in Daddy's chest that says, I'm not needed there. A tenseness in Daddy's chest that says, that love no longer lives there. I hold my Daddy even tighter and I bury my face into his chest even farther and I rock him to the side…to the side…to the side, and I say, "I love you, Daddy. No matter what you think of me, I still love you."

You see, Mama has always taught me to have a little bit of pride about myself, no matter how much it hurts. So I jerk away from that chest. And I take one last look at those killer eyes and I run and I run and I don't ever want to stop running. Because if I do, I just know that the pain is going to tap me on the shoulder, and the hurt is going to explode in my chest.

Just then I hear the crackling of thunder, and I look up just in time to see a fork of lightning stabbing at the sky and a heavy rain spills upon the pavement and I don't want to run anymore. I just want to stand here and let the rain wash away my tears, wash against my face, my arms and my legs. But you see the rain can't get at my pain, a pain that's rooted somewhere underneath my childhood.

The rain sure can't wash away my pain, but it washes away something else, that very night….my childhood. I catch a glimpse of it sliding along the side of the gutter, and it slides right down into the sewer too, never to be seen again.

"Annie Mae….Annie Mae," I hear Mama's voice tearing through the rain drops. At first I want to run, but I don't. I'm too grown for that now and whatever stew Mama has cooked up for me, I'm gonna eat it. She runs towards me wearing a black, shiny rain coat and slinging my rain coat across one arm and carrying a blue umbrella in the other.

She cocks her head and looks at me all strange like and says, "Girl what's wrong with yoou? Don't you know you can catch your death out heah? Acting all crazy and knocking my good piece down and running away from the house like that? What's wrong with yoou?" she asks, while helping me on with my coat.

"I'm sorry Mama, for knocking your phoenix down and when we get home I'll be ready for my whipping."

Again Mama cocks her head and looks at me real strange like and says, "That's alright, Baby, you didn't hurt nothing no how. You just chipped the beak, that's all and you mean more to me than that old phoenix ever could. And if listening to soul music means that much to you, you go on and listen to it. Don't make any sense for nobody to get all wiled up over some damn shoo-bop-de-bop mess. Don't make any kinda sense. And it sure in the hell ain't worth it either." I knew that was the closest I would ever come to getting an apology from Mama.

"You mean that Mama," I ask.

"As sure as I mean to stay black," Mama says.

And I look up at Mama, and I get to thinking, that for Mama, life has been a pot of greens. What I mean is, sometimes after your greens are all washed and cut up you put them in the pot and it seems like you got a whole mess of greens, more greens than you can ever eat yourself and once those same greens start to boiling and simmering you stick your head back down in that pot and it ain't hardly nothing at the bottom. That's what I think Mama did. She stuck her head, back down in that pot and saw it wasn't hardly no life floating around at the bottom. So she latches on to me and my life and my pot of greens, hoping there's enough in that pot for the both of us to share.

I cut my eyes at Mama and say, "I saw Daddy."

"Hmm….Hmmmm, what did that no good bastard have to say for himself?"

Now, maybe I'm wrong but despite Mama's words, seems like I hear a strand of hope floating around in the back of them, so I swallow in a large piece of breath and I say, "He still loves you very much, Mama, and me and Gloria too. He says he's growing tired of that street life and that he'll be coming home real soon, you'll see."

"Girl, you lying like a Persian rug," Mama says, with a wave of her hand.

"Ugh….ugh, Mama if I'm lying I'm flying." And again I cut my eyes at Mama and I say, "He held me Mama. He held me so tight till I thought that I was gonna bust into a million pieces. And then Mama he cupped his hands to my face and he bent down and kissed me on my forehead, and Mama, when he did that I felt like a princess." And Mama looks down at me and smiles then.

As we continue to walk home rain drops beat down upon Mama's blue umbrella and Mama takes hold of my hand. I'm feeling much too grown for Mama to be holding my hand, especially out in the streets. But I don't protest or nothing, I just let her squeeze it and eventually I sort of give her hand a little squeeze too.

After that night, my heart becomes a hunter. It looks for love, the kind of love that the drugstore sells for 10 cents in those romance comic books. I'm talking about the love between a man and a woman. My father didn't love me, so my heart went looking for a man that would. To this day, my heart continues to look for love.

Part IV

Circa 1969

You know, life is full of tricks, and traveling down life's highway can be a funny, funny thing and if you're not careful all the jokes will be on YOU. Sometimes, when you think you're going, you're really coming. What I mean is you think you're running from something and the thing you're running from is far, far behind you and you think you're traveling down this straight path, but if you don't watch where you're going and you dilly-dally, that very road will curve and swerve. The very thing you're running from will stare you dead smack in the face. I know because it happened to my Daddy and if you're not careful it can happen to YOU!

When the word got around about Daddy, gossip flew around town, like a swarm of locusts. As a matter of fact, people still joke about it on the north side. They say that child was the hottest thing going since cayenne pepper. And as the old folks would say, that girl was built like a brick shit house! Now she was only nineteen years old at the time, but they say that child knew more about sex than the Kama Sutra. It was also said that child could do things with her body that weren't humanly possible! Men would line up outside her door like poor folks to a soup kitchen.

Well, Daddy was obviously looking for a taste of strange fruit that night and this time he bit off so much he gagged on it. They say Daddy's strange fruit came in the shape and form of Reba Henshaw, and right in the middle of the act, Daddy's eyes get as big as golf balls, his body starts to herking and jerking and every time he tries to roll over his entire body gets as stiff as drywall, and poor Reba starts to wailing so loud you could hear her in the halls of Montezuma, trying to get that man up off her. She's trying her damnest to untangle her arms and legs from his body to reach the phone on the bed stand.

And the more she struggles the farther she slides underneath that man. Do you know, that by the time the ambulance got there, that child had just about suffocated under that man(now you know, those paramedics had a good time talking about her and calling her everything but a child of God) and do you know that girl became a *Jehovah Witness* after the night? You can see that girl a many a day, standing at the train station spreading the word of the Gospel, and handing out the *Watch Tower*. You see, Reba Henshaw found religion that Christmas Eve night, and my Daddy found Hell, his in his Christmas stocking. Now my father, for all intents and purposes isn't an old man at the time, he's just 41 years old, but I guess all that womanizing, drinking, carousing and fast food eating had gotten the best of him. He has a stroke in the arms of another woman. Oh yes, my father found hell that night, and Selma Louise Jenkins, be thy name.

It's early Christmas morning and a gray, creepy darkness has its hold on the sky. There isn't a snow flake to be found and you know nothing good can come out of something this dismal looking. I hear the phone ring, but Mama picks it up. It's Grant Hospital, and Daddy has been admitted. Mama takes everything in that the receiver is saying. She nods her head, twists her mouth and taps her feet. She slams the phone down and looks at me and says, in a matter of fact way, "Get your clothes on and wake up Gloria; yo Daddy is in the hospital." So I hurry up and do what she says. But all the while I'm doing a Helen Keller number, feeling around, trying my best to read her mood, but I can't for the life of me.

When we get to the hospital it's like a swarm of activity, nurses in white caps and dresses with charts in their hands, flinging from one room and flying into the next. There are sleepy eyed interns with their stethoscopes slinging from their necks hustling from one code blue and bustling to the next. Garland stretches from the walls. Christmas trees grace secure corners wishing one and all Christmas Cheer. Holiday music floats through the halls, advising, "Have yourself a merry little Christmas".

The three of us head for the Nurses' Station. When Mama introduces herself and tells who she's there to see, the young nurse smothers a laugh, eyes a near-by intern, and then turns as red as a stop light, while she points to Daddy's room. Mama raises her head a little bit higher, clings to her purse a little bit tighter, and she smiles at the girl with hooded, knowing eyes and with a slight nod she says, "Thank you." Do you know, that nurse takes a hard swallow on that laugh and even grabs her throat?

It's as if Mama is saying, "You're young yet Baby. Oh, but keep on living and see the many surprises that await YOU, down this road called life live and see Baby. All you gotta do is live and see." Now I hear a slim sprinkle of laughter when our backs are turned, but I doubt if it came from THAT nurse.

When we enter Daddy's room a thin sheet of light comes from the window and lays across Daddy's bed. This once big, robust man looks like a shriveled up lump in that bed with a lop-sided head poking out at the top. There wasn't one wrinkle in those white, crisp sheets. They fold neatly across Daddy's chest. His right arm flops straight down and the other arm forms a "u" across his chest. Daddy's mouth droops on one side and his chin is wet from the constant drooling.

He opens his eyes as he senses our presence. His eyes dart from Gloria, me and finally, Mama…Mama. His eyes lay on Mama, like the sheets on his bed. Mama bends over and kisses his droopy jaw. His stiff head searches for Mama's eyes, and then he whimpers like a whipped puppy. "Mmmm…mmmm…mm..mm…mmmm."

Mama smiles at him now, and she massages his head and whispers, "Shhh, it's alright, Baby…I forgive you. Hush, now, hush," His limp head reaches for Mama's chest as best as he can and shameful tears roll down my Daddy's cheeks. Mama has said those three mighty words, "I forgive you." I think at this moment, he needs to hear those words, more than he needs breath in his body and as best as he can, he takes his limp hand and reaches for Mama's hand and Mama squeezes it and looks over at me and smiles that warm as buttermilk biscuits smile.

The next day or so, Mama meets with the social worker. She's a perky little thing, fresh out of Grad School, with fresh ideas of making the world a better place. Her chili red hair and robin blue suit are as bouncy as she is. She tells Mama that with Daddy working for the railroad and all, he can be placed in a good, quality care facility. Because he has a good pension and Mama wouldn't have to worry about his health care cost. Mama looks at that social worker with cold, glaring eyes and says," I want to be near my husband, so I can visit him everyday and I want him in a private room."

Why yes, of course, that's exactly what I had in mind," she says, all bubbly like, and talking with her hands." Somewhere overlooking the lake, with pleasant surroundings, and with bright, happy colors," she says crossing her legs, and leaning forward with enthusiasm. Daddy eyes those legs with enthusiasm. Mama eyes him with cruelty.

"I've already made arrangements for him to stay at the Regal Nursing home," says Mama.

The social worker sucks in her breath and gawks at Mama. "Maybe, you don't understand, Mrs. Jenkins, but that nursing facility has been under state investigation for the past year. It's not suitable for---"

"It's what I THINK is suitable," says Mama, waving her finger in the woman's face and slitting her eyes. "Do YOU understand?"

The social worker watches Mama's finger like a tennis ball, then slits her green eyes back at Mama and flashes them over at Daddy and then back at Mama. "Yes, I understand," she says in a defeated voice. "I DO understand." And I wonder if she understands for the first time that you may be able to change things in this world, but you sure as hell can't change the people. You see people are molded in a plaster called time, and only they and God have the power to change---themselves.

The first time I set foot in that nursing home, I 'm as confused as that poor social worker. Mama has dropped Daddy off on the South Side of hell. The walls are cracking, peeling and chipping and just waiting on the floor like bread crumbs, inviting some poor, confused resident to come along and grab up a taste.

One old lady hobbles over towards me, begging for help. "Buggala (Yiddish for little lamb)," she says, "Can you please help me find my daughter? Surely, if she knew I was here, she would come and get me. Please, help me" and I bet you my neck; it was her very daughter who delivered her to the devil. Her hair is matted to her head and her clothes look like she has done everything in them but pray.

The smell…the smell of urine clings to the floors and the walls like a shroud to a dead man. I tell you, when I walk through the halls, I know the taste and smell of poverty.

When we open the door to Daddy's room, it smells like a zoo up in there! And the funk has my nose in a cat fight! DIRT…. DIRT….DIRT, every crack, corner, shelf, window and roach is full of dirt. Now I'm not talking about ordinary dust here, I'm talking about crust. That room is so filthy; it would take a river of bleach to clean it up.

Daddy is sitting up in the wheelchair, and only God and a stop watch know how long he's been sitting there. He sees me and Mama and starts to whimpering, "Mmmm…mmm…mmmm." His food is sitting on the table, waiting for some nurse or aide to be Christian enough to come along and feed him. I go over and feel it and the pureed food is so cold, it's gotten hard and jells on the sides.

You know, I may be dumb, I may be stupid, but I'm not hooked on crazy. You see, it's payback time for Daddy. They say payback is a dog. But, you see, this particular dog is a pit bull and it's teeth have clamped down into Daddy's behind, and it isn't about to let go.

Mama pops her hips towards Daddy, and takes his hand, "Hey Baby, hey Sugar," she says, and pops a kiss on his jaw.

"Mmmmm….mmmm….mmm," he says protesting and jerking his arm.

"Ahhh Sugar, everything's alright."

One of the aides walks in. Now, this particular aide, she hadn't seen me, but I sure as hell have seen her, when we first walked in. She had the unmitigated gall to be in an OPEN room with a gin bottle to her head. And this heifer wants to give care to somebody? She had better step back, and give care to herself….First. "You want me ta feed your husband?" she asks my mother (seems to me she should have thought about that two hours ago).

Mama gets a good whiff of her breath, smiles with squinted eyes and says, "Naw, Baby, that's alright. Me and my daughter will take care of everything," Mama says, pulling a $5.00 bill from her purse. Heah," she pushes the bill into the aide's hands. "Have lunch on me, today"

"Oh why, thank you ma'am, that sure is nice of you."

"Hmmm….Hmmmmm," says Mama, pushing her out the already open door.

Mama slams that door then. She slams that door so hard that the echo vibrates against the window, and then rings across the silverware and chinks the glasses upon the table. Me and Daddy gulp in a deep breath of silence, then….Mama swirls around like a witch casting a spell. She folds her arms, taps her heels on the floor and slices up Daddy with machete eyes.

"Annie Mae," she says, not taking her eyes off Daddy, "Stand by the door….and make sure nobody comes up in this motha fucka."

Now, I stare at her, for what seems like a long, long time. And I haven't even made up my mind, if I want to go along with this madness that's just about to pop off. But my feet have already made up their minds. Before I can say, "Ten Hut," they are marching over towards the door.

Mama whips that wheelchair around like a jump rope, and stares Daddy right in the face, "You low down, dirty motha fucka, son of a bitch. You left me, for nine long years, MOTHA FUCKA! I waited for you, with hunger pangs in my stomach, fear in the back of my throat, and a 5 day notice in my hand, I waited for YOU, for nine long years. I just loved you and waited for you. Nine long years, I had to raise and fend for our two girls the best that I could. THE BEST THAT I COULD! You were only 5 blocks away….5 blocks away, motha fucka. You think, I didn't know? And you couldn't even drop by and drop a dime in my pocket. And I didn't even DREAM about filing for child support, or getting a divorce, because I thought sooner or later your conscience would come knocking at my front door. Oooh but I was wrong, I was as wrong as a cup with no bottom. And I went to the bank, and I just KNEW you had left me a little something. But you had cleaned me out didn't ya motha fucka? You had cleaned me out like the goddamn board of health. And after ALLLL of that I still loved you and I still waited for YOU….I waited for YOU! Oh but after alll of that I still made it, didn't I motha fucka?

"Gloria is in her second year of college now, down there in Dekalb, Illinois. She's studying to be a teacher. I did that for her motha fucka, not YOU! ME….ME! You were too busy whore hopping. Annie Mae over there, your baby girl, remember her? She's a freshman now, at the HIGH SCHOOL FOR PERFORMING ARTS. She had to audition to get in. Oh yes, but with all of the lessons I shell out for, she knew what to do and how to do it. She made it. Oh yes she made it, on her way to becoming an opera singer. And you know who made all of that possible, motha fucka? Me….Me!" she says, pounding her hand on her chest. "While you were out there ho' chasing, sniffing and slobbering and giving your money to every skirt that pops in yo face, I STILL MADE IT! Through the storm and through the rain, I made it. And I done found my sunshine. I made it, motha fucka….ahhh…I made it! And now that you're all crippled up, and broken up, you're ready to come on back to me. Am I right? What can you do for me?" she asks, sizing him up. "Shiiit, you can't even offer me up a prayer. And if ya think for one damn minute that I'm sending you to a better nursing home, ya lying….like St. Peter on Jesus. If that's yo dream Baby, I'm sorry you ever woke up. I'm keeping that extra cash, goddammit, to add to my nest egg!"

She cocks her head then, and stares at him with a glimmer in her eye. "And you know what caused all this trouble? Wait a minute, I'll show ya." Mama stomps over to the window sill and plucks out a pair of plastic gloves from a box. She puts them on with two loud pops…POP…POP. And she stomps back over to Daddy again.

"Mmmmm……Mmmmmmmmmm," Daddy looks at me with begging eyes and a trembling body. I cast my eyes to the floor and watch a mouse scamper by.

Mama whips up Daddy's hospital gown and says, "This is the trouble, ahh this is the trouble, right heah y'all!" and she twist and pulls on that man, like salt water taffy.

Daddy starts to shaking his body and waving his limp hand. I stare at the floor, the walls, anything but those begging eyes. I know I should have stopped it. God knows I should have stopped it. But I couldn't stop the pain of wanting to be held by my father. I couldn't stop the tears that lull me to sleep each night. I couldn't stop from wanting his love. So why should I stop his pain? He sure as hell didn't stop mine!

Now, I know, you're probably criticizing me and chastising me. But before you condemn me for being a monster, you better check out your own monsters. I bet you got them buried so deep, you would have to unlock the cellars of hell to get at them. But bring them on out. And I want you to take a good, long look at them, before you start condemning me for my wrong-doing.

"Mmmm…mmmm….mmmmm," Daddy cries.

"Ahhh Baby, ahh Honey, don't whimper now sugar. You didn't whimper when I didn't know where our next soda cracker was coming from, now did ya? So don't whimper now Baby, because this party is just getting started!"

Then Mama stomps into the bathroom and starts singing an old time spiritual at the top of her lungs, *"Thine will be done….too much trouble in this world…. too much trouble in this world. I'm going home to live with my God."* And she's banging and clanging around in that bathroom something fierce.

"Mm…Mm..Mm..Mmmm," he cries, shaking the wheelchair, back and forward.

And I ignore my Daddy's cries and I ignore his needs, the way he has ignored mine.

Mama comes out of that bathroom with a steel bed pan and a soaking wet bath towel, and the smell of alcohol burns through the room. Mama wrings the towel into the pan. Then she lifts that alcohol soaked towel over her shoulder and…POP…POP…POP. She whips Daddy with that very towel, while I stand and watch. I stand and WATCH. And I do nothing.

They say when you whip a person with an alcohol soaked towel that it stings like the devil. And it doesn't leave a trace or a scar of the punishment. Oh, but you see, I wear the scars. I wear the scars on my mind like a scarlet letter.

After each pop, Daddy's body jerks and flops and curves to the side. Then he gives a feeble wave at the towel," Mmmm…. mmmmm….mmmmmm." And he shakes his head, as if he's crying out for mercy or crying out in disbelief, that this could possibly be happening to him.

When Mama finishes, Daddy has slumped all the way down in the wheelchair. And tear drops lay on the floor tile, like checkers on a checker board. Mama grabs hold of that wheelchair again and stares Daddy in his eyes. He turns his face from her as best as he can. She holds it up and steadies it in her hand. Mama's eyes swell up with hate and she says, "I want you to curl up and die. I want you to curl up like the maggot you are and die. You hear me? You black maggot motha fucka you!" and she jerks his head as hard as she can to the side. So hard you can almost hear it snap.

Daddy strains then, to push his body up straight and he turns his lop-sided head toward Mama. He works his jaws good and hard. Daddy gathers up his spirit and his gumption and tries to spit in Mama's face….to spit in Mama's face!

But the weak, silver strand doesn't do nothing. It just meets with his chin and drips down his hospital gown.

Mama laughs then, a deep, mannish laugh and says, "You can't get through me motha fucka...You gotta wake up at 5:00 in the morning, crawl through a barb wire fence and roll down a hill of razor blades to get through this!" she pats her hand on her chest.

"Come on Annie Mae, let's blow this hell hole," Mama says, shaking back her curls and smoothing out her dress. Daddy's body shakes like a generator, he hangs his twisted head deeper into his chest, and cries, cries, cries. Only, that wasn't my Daddy in that chair anymore, it's a man with a death sentence.

A day or two later there's a concert ticket for the Isley Brothers on my pillow. It was a silent reward for a silent crime. Every time we go to visit Daddy at the nursing home I stand watch. And every time I stand watch there is a tape deck on my night stand, a new dress in my closet, a new watch in my jewelry box. And each time, the crime becomes easier and the rewards greater.

It's gotten to the point whenever me and Mama visit him, before he gets too bad off, he will see us coming and start twisting his limp hand to knock things over and whimpering as loud as he can. One time, he's rocking so hard he nearly topples over his wheelchair and lands on the floor. But no one ever seems to pay poor Daddy any attention. Thinking back now, I wonder, is it because the staff is too busy with other things, or too busy collecting Mama's money?

Well, anyway, Mama will put spit into Daddy's food and force him to eat it. And if he even looks like he would spit it out, she'll clamp his mouth together with one hand and massage his throat with the other, until he has swallowed every drop. You see Mama has a pot of boiling hate for that man. And she has seasoned that pot with the three D's decadence, deceit and demise!

Daddy does just what Mama told him to do too. Over a period of time that man curls up and gnarls up just like a maggot. Eventually, he gets so curled up he can't sit up in the wheelchair anymore. His knees meet up with his chin, and both hands criss-cross around his chest like a mummy. So he stays in bed now. And he waits and waits on the mercy and kindness of others. His stomach waits, his bed sores wait, his diaper…waits.

That mercy and kindness usually comes from Gloria, she visits Daddy whenever she comes home from school, which isn't too often. But when she's home she cares for Daddy the best she can. She bathes him, feeds him, and tries to massage his gnarled up limbs.

Each visit must take a lot out of Gloria. Because she comes home raising more hell than a wet cat. She tears into the house, hoping, hollering and crying. And she and Mama would tear into each other and turn the joint out with their arguments. And if Mama doesn't want to hear anymore, she turns her back on Gloria and starts washing dishes or mopping the floor. And to the top of her lungs she sings another spiritual, "Oh my Father, is the pilot on this plane. Yes he is. And he knows that his child is on board." You see, Gloria wants Daddy placed in a better facility. And Mama….well, we know what Mama wants.

By Gloria being 5 years older than me, she remembers when Daddy was a real Daddy. That's an experience I've never tasted. That night, after I went looking for Daddy, I looked up in the closet and I pull down an old, dusty photo album. I know that the truth lies in those pages, like a picture in a frame. And I find all sorts of yellowed, frayed-at-the-end photos of Daddy holding Gloria, holding Gloria on her first birthday, holding Gloria at the zoo, holding Gloria at Christmas, holding Gloria at Halloween. And they are always throwing their heads back and laughing into each others eyes. They share a secret, a secret that is only shared by a daughter and a beloved father.

But do you know that I flip through those pages and flip back again? And I can't find one single, damn picture of him holding me? Not one! Oh, I tell you, I would have walked from here to the catacombs of hell, to have found one picture of me and my Daddy, a picture of me sitting on his lap, and with my head touching the crispness of his work shirt. My arms would wrap loosely around his shoulders and my feet dangling above his big feet. And he would hold me by my waist and his eyes would rest upon my eyes. And his eyes would say….his eyes would say, "This is my Baby Girl, and I'm proud."

I find an old photograph of Daddy. He looks to be about nineteen or twenty, at the time, And he's standing alone, at what looks like an army base, and he's wearing fatigues. I slip it out of the plastic cover, I take to into the bathroom, and I flick on the light to examine my face, good and hard, in the mirror, because the mirror doesn't lie. His eyes are big and round. My eyes are small and sloped. His nose is broad on top and narrow at the bottom. My nose is broad from top to bottom. His cheek bones sit high and sharp. My cheek bones sit flat and hallow.

I went home that night, when I was twelve, after finding my daddy, I kneel by my bed and I prayed my twelve year old prayer's to God. I ask him to send me the truth a twelve year old's truth, because I can't ask my mother, and expect to keep my teeth in my mouth. "Am I really this man's child God? Is my mother wrapping me in a blanket of lies? Does Daddy know that I'm not his child? Is that why he rejects me? Show me the way, God, show me the truth!" I fall asleep on my knees that night, with my head propped up on the side of the pillow and my hands still folded. When I awakened that following morning, God hasn't sent me the truth, only a stiff neck.

The nurses and the aides don't turn Daddy like they're supposed to. And he gets this big sore on his behind. Now, I'm not going to sit here and lie. That sore was so big you can make your whole fist a home in it! And still have enough room to move around. Well, it's about this time that daddy starts wearing a catheter bag for his urine. Do you know that Mama pours urine into Daddy's sore, so it can get infected? And again I stand by. And again, I watch, and again I'm the silent partner in a silent crime.

And Daddy gets to the point where he doesn't whimper or nothing when he sees me and Mama coming. I tell you, he just lays there and takes it. He takes Mama's hell, with a napkin of dignity and a fork of courage. I think, towards the end it sort of scares Mama too. Because she'll be working her sho-nuf evil on that man (some terrible, terrible things that I don't even want to say) and he burns his eyes straight into hers. Then without batting an eye and without straining a muscle he takes his droopy lips and curves them up (just a little bit) and smiles a twisted smile and winks at Mama.

Looking back on it now, sometimes I think, laying crippled up and twisted up in that bed, that Daddy has found something, something that has been lost for a long, long time....his manhood. And Mama sees it too. Because every time he gives her that look, she jumps, drops whatever prop of destruction she's using, and shakes like a hula dancer. I think she likes it better when he fights. It gives her more power.

And then his eyes will roam and search me out. I can always feel his eyes on me. Eyes that make me wonder if I have a conscience, eyes that surely think that if I have one, I would have put a stop to Mama's madness long ago. But you see I DON'T stop the madness, so maybe I DON'T have a conscience. But God has a conscience. And he delivers Daddy, from Mama's madness. After three years, of floating in a cesspool of hell, Daddy dies. I know and now, you know, that me and Mama killed that man, just as if we have pushed a knife through his throat…we killed that man. Me and Mama never talk about what really happened to Daddy. We are silent partners, in a silent crime.

Part V

Circa l971

"I ain't having no abortion, Mama! And there ain't nothing you can do about it," I shout, while shaking my hips to the slamming, jamming rhythm of the radio. Sly and the Family Stone is instructing me to, *"Dance to the Music."* I'm 16 years old now, and on this muggy, musty August afternoon, flies are diving through the kitchen like fighter pilots.

And I'm dishing out hell to Mama on a silver platter. The day I stepped foot into my adolescence was the day I stepped foot into the valley of the hellion bitches. All of her "Ma Dear" glitter and shine has been sandpapered away. I'm not afraid of her anymore. And I have learned to whip her up a daily batch of rebellion, with a side order of arrogance. And around every corner there is another lump of heartache for her to swallow. What could she do? She had threatened several times to put me into a home for wayward girls. But hey, in the immortal words of Jerry lee Lewis, "I'm still waiting, Honey!" It's gotten to the point where the only thing she can tell me is the limit on her credit cards (or at least that's what I tell myself).

A few days before, Gloria my sister, had sped off for her senior year at Northern Illinois University, in a brand new Pinto and I wouldn't realize until later how much I need her to make a mad turn in that Pinto and lend me some advice and a cup of sympathy.

I cut my eyes at Mama, and prance over to the kitchen table and flip up the volume full blast. And I bend over and stick my booty out. I slap my hands on my behind, and I do a low-down, hutti-gutti, smutti- gutti dance, called…defiance. The humping and thumping of my right hip says, "ugh…ugh…ugh…ugh…you can't tell me what to do."

While the bumping and pumping of my left hip says, "Hmmmp…hmmmp…hmmmp…this is my life, and I'll live it as I want to…hmmmp…hmmmp…hmmmp," Mama narrows her eyes, and shoots pass me, and snatches the radio out of the socket, and hurls it into the dish water…SPLASH! The radio bobs up and down in the suds. A wave of soapy bubbles slams onto the floor, and rips and drips across the walls.

Mama circles me, with bullets in her eyes and fire in her stride. She waves her index finger in my face, and says, "You see this finger? Down South we call this the bad luck finger. And Bitch I'd rather see you dead, and watch you go blind, than for you to think for one damn minute that you're gonna lay up in MY house and be a goddamn breeding factory. 'Cause just and sho' as ya gap ya legs open for one, you'll gap ya legs open for twenty one. And I ain't having it Bitch! Do ya heah me? I'll fry onions in hell befo' I have it!" Mama folds her arms and says, "Hump, when I was yo age, I knew as much about a man as a dog knows about Sunday School."

"Yeah, but you sure knew how to pump a man full of bullet holes, and leave him for dead now didn't ya," I ask.

Mama jerks her head, as if I have slapped the mess outta her. She had no idea that Big Mama has unloaded her past on me, like a nuclear waste dump. "What---What, you say?" she ask.

"Miss Woman pleeze, you heard me. I didn't stutter," I say, shaking my head.

Then she frowns her face up something awful, like she's sucking on a sour lemon. And she whips that same finger back into my face and says, "Bitch, I'll kill ya, I'll kill ya dead. Don't you ever, as long as God gives you breath in yo body, talk about me, my life and my past. I've lived a good life, Bitch. And I've got a mighty fine bank account, and a sho nuf nice home ta sho for it." I toss my hand, and I turn to make my exit.

Mama grabs my hand and spins me around like a yo-yo and says, "Ya think ya grown now, don't ya? Ya done gone and made a pure-dee slut outta yo'sef. Hmmmp,he doesn't want you now, Baby. He wouldn't want yooou, if you were the next, Pam Damn Grier. He done used ya up and thrown ya away like a busted condom, Honey. And what ya got ta sho for it, huh? But a heartache, a wet ass and a belly full of trouble. Ahhh, but ya grown now, ain't ya? Well, let's just see how grown ya really are…get the fuck outta my house!" she says. "You heard me, I said hit the Boulevard, Bitch," Mama says, opening up the hallway door with one hand and shoving me out with the other.

And my world becomes a blur of water colors, because I can't believe that Mama is doing this to me. I frown and look at her, as if she's lost her ever-loving mind.

"Okay, okay Mama, I'll leave. Just give me a chance to get my clothes, and my summer job money together. I'll leave Mama. Just give me a few minutes," I say patting my hands against the air. Now, I want you to know, that at this point, I would say or do anything to hold on to my precious baby. And isn't that the way of a mother? And I'm thinking by my juvenile calculations, that I'm only three months along. But I'm as far from that as a saint is from the devil.

"Hell naw, Bitch! You came through me naked, and goddammit, you gone leave through me…NAKED." She claws for my T-shirt and I try to jerk away and spin around, but it's too late…popopopopopopop, Mama, rips that T- shirt off my back, with my bra to boot! With a twisted smile, she twirls the bra around, like she's performing a strip-tease. I look at my bra, I look at her, and my mouth flies open and my pride slips out. I cup my breasts and make a run for the house.

Then, with a vicious thud…BOOM! Mama topples me, like a pot of hot, angry grits, to the hallway floor. She tightens her lips and flames her eyes into mine. She tears open my jeans and commences to pull them off and my pink panties too. I'm grabbing hold of her hands now, and snatching up my panties at the same time. "Don't you ever grab hold of my hands, Bitch, I'll kill ya!" Mama blares. And I'm scuffling and huffing to save what's left of my pride and my panties.

She stops then, and an eerie calm washes over her face and she's breathing like a prize fighter. And there's stillness in the air. And I can hear the pied piper song of the ice cream truck outside. I take in a deep breath of relief. A smile warms Mama's face. She looks down at my panties and up into my face. Again she smiles, looking down at my panties and up into my---I widen my eyes and my mind, and I roll anyway but the right way, trying to get out of HER way. She catches me by the side of my panties and the waistband begins to pop and unravel. Mama ropes that loose elastic around her hand, and lassoes me right back in, like Wild Bill Hickock. An evil laugh gushes from Mama's mouth, "Haa…Haaagh!"

And I roll and kick my legs into a frantic tizzy, screaming, "AAAAAAAHHHHHRIGHT…OKAAAY…OKAAAY!"

She sips in a deep breath of satisfaction, smiles at me with victorious eyes and let's go of me with a powerful thump. I try to bunch my pride and my panties back together, while pulling my jeans over my hips. But the situation gets the best of me, and a cloud of shame pays me a visit.

You see, Mama wants to be my everything. But doesn't she understand that I have to make my own decisions, my own mistakes? And dammit if I do fall, please God, give me the good sense to be strong enough, and adult enough, to get right back up on my own two feet…MY OWN two feet. And try it one more time, with a little bit more feeling, and a little bit more effort. Why couldn't she understand that? Why couldn't she just let go?

"Okay Mama, I'll have the abortion," I say, as tears scream down my face. I wave my fist and yell; "I'll have the abortion!" Where else was I going to go? What else was I going to do? The baby's father had made it as clear as ice water, that I was just the morsel of the month. But we'll talk more about that later.

Now you know that in the early seventies, abortions were taboo here, in the State of Illinois. Most doctors would avoid them like a leper colony. I heard tell of this one well respected doctor, who tried to help so many young girls at that time and was stabbed to death… 51 times. And he is found bound and gagged in the trunk of his Mercedes Benz, with his hands chopped off. And they say the killer dipped his finger in that good doctor's blood and writes," Baby Killer", on his forehead. But to me the most frightening thing about it was that when they pulled the duct tape from his mouth, they find a fetus stuffed down that man's throat. And do you know that to this day they can't find the killer? So that man's secret profession turns out to be his deadly profession.

So like I said, at the time if a girl wants an abortion, she only has a few options. She can fly to New York (which a lot of the well-to-do girls do at school). She can meet up with a back alley meat grinder. Or she can become best friends with a wire hanger.

Mama stays kneeling on the floor for a long, long time, rubbing her hands against her knees, and looking up at the ceiling, as if she's searching for answers to unasked questions. She bites down on her lower lip real hard like, and takes in a long breath and says," I'm gone tell you something, Annie Mae, something that nobody knows but me and my Jesus. You were five years old at the time, and yo Daddy had just… up and left. And I find out that I'm pregnant. Hmmmmp, you talking about something that knocks me for a loop? I thought I was going when I was coming, because I was always so careful about that sorta thing. And ooh I guess I'm about six weeks along. And I would sell hot peppers in hell befo I bring another crumb snatcher into this heah world. Now, I don't know where yo Daddy is, or if and when he's coming back. And I sho as hell ain't about ta look him up ta find out…And here's my right hand ta God," she says, pointing her hand towards heaven. "I climb up on the top of the refrigerator, and I throw myself off." Mama slaps her hand on her thigh and shouts, "I throw myself off!" A wave of silence fills the room, a silence that pokes at my belly and gets caught in my throat. She eyes a piece of lint on the carpet and says, "When I hit the floor a pain rips through my stomach, like lightening to a beam pole. I limp into the bathroom and I sit down on the toilet. And I wait…wait for the truth. When I flush the toilet, and the ball of blood bubbles up to the top and circles round and round…and…then… down…I know, I did my job, and did it well." Just then Mama lets out a long awaited sigh, and she looks up at the ceiling one more time and lifts one knee and then the other, and makes her way into the house…a house of pain…a house of secrets.

I cry, I lay on that floor, in that hallway half naked, and I cry. I cry for myself. I cry for all of the unborn babies of the world, the babies that will never run home from school, waving a white sheet of paper like a flag, shouting, "Look Mommy, look! I got an A on my math test." And their Mommies will never praise them with a mountain of hugs and kisses. I cry for all of the unborn babies in the world who will never wake up Christmas morning, with their eyes screaming with delight, "Look Mommy look, Santa brought me a bicycle for Christmas. He knew just what I wanted, Mommy, Santa knew." And the joy will be so contagious; the mother's eyes will well up with tears. I cry for all of the unborn babies in the world. The babies that were meant to be, but will never have the chance…to be. Their unforgiving souls live in a dusty corner of their mother's minds. Their gray, bloated bodies float in a sea of lies and secrets.

I heard my mama cry tonight. For the first time in my life, I heard my mama cry. And my mama is as strong as five gladiators. When she calls the hospital two years ago to check up on Big Mama's condition, the nurse tells her that Big Mama is dead. That woman doesn't shed a tear…not one tear. She just grabs hold of the kitchen table, and plops herself down in a chair. And she cradles that dead phone to her chest, like she's holding on to a big piece of heartache. ERRRRRRRRRRRRRR…Just a rocking…Just a cradling that dead phone. And she stays that way for a long, long time… ERRRRRRRRRRRRRRRRR…She stares off, into a space called nothing. But she doesn't cry. She doesn't shed a tear.

But oh she lays in that bed, and she cries now. She asks her God, if He is a just God, and a true God, how can He allow this horrible thing to happen to her child. You see, her God,ain't the same as my God, because my God ain't no damn baby killer.

"Why Lawd, why? Why did you let this happen,ta MY CHILD, Jesus? You know I tried to raise her right, Jesus. You know I DID! I ain't never had no bunch of men around my daughters, Jesus…You know, I didn't. Why Jesus…WHY? All my hopes, Lawd, ALLLLL my dreams. they're gone now, Jesus…GONE!" Mama sniffs on a few pieces of her heart ache and says, "Show me the way, Jesus. Lead me down your path to righteousness. Show me the way, Jesus. Lead me, Lawd…Lead me!"

I lie in my bed, in the next room, listening to her moaning and suffering. And the child in me wants to run to my mother and lay her head on my night gown. And let my night gown soak up all of her pain. And I want to rub her back and say, "Don't cry Mama, it'll be alright, you'll see." Because no child wants to see their mothers cry or suffer…no child.

Oh, but that hellion in me…that bitch in me…declines. The hellion bitch in me wants to see that witch's pain…wants to see a green gush of pain…a Niagara Falls of pain…wants her to grasp for her breath, come up seven times and drown in that pain.

The hellion bitch in me wants to jump into her room and scream over her pain, "Cry Bitch, cry! Cry me a goddamn fountain!"

The following night Mama and me slip into the back of a cab. Mama has set me up on a date with a meat grinder. But what, I couldn't figure out, for the life of me is… why? Hmmmp,the woman has money, she wasn't hurting for no duckets. They didn't call her Selma "Lawsuit" Jenkins for nothing. She can book me on a red eye flight to New York City in a heart beat. Is she that cheap? Is she that selfish? These thoughts rumble through my mind as I lay my head against the back seat and watch the street lights stream across the sky. And my body jerks this way and that way as the cabbie hits one pot hole after another.

But you see, it doesn't really matter, because in my mind my baby is already dead, and I'm dead too. It isn't really me in the back of that cab anyway. It's a zombie…see? And I'm trapped inside of its shell. Mama sits beside me, just a smiling and squeezing my hand, trying to console me. But how the hell can you console the dead?

Mama smiles that warm as buttermilk biscuits smile, that smile she always smiles when she gets her way. Her eyes narrow, her mouth puckers, and her cheeks lift. And I wish to almighty God that she was dead! I want her to keel over and die, like a cockroach drowning in Black Flag. And for good measure I'd take a shovel and conk her in the head a couple of times. Then I'd take that same shovel and heave a pile of dirt and spray it in her face. And I would scream, "Die Bitch, die!" And I'd smack that dirt down, and I'd pat that dirt down. Until that witch was firm and tight and good and dead, in her GRAVE!

The driver pulls into the Pilsen Neighborhood, somewhere around 25th and Ashland. The streets are littered with children. The girls are playing double Dutch, and the boys are playing stick ball. On the other side of the street, I spot a bunch of teenagers nesting out on the stoop, drinking wine, passing a joint from one pair of dream-weaving lips to the next. A nearby fire hydrant was left on from the heat of the day. It pours their dreams down into the sewer.

The engine cuts off and dies in front of a small, frame house with a long staircase. Loud Salsa music spills from the house. The kind of lip-smacking, heart-thumping, sexual beat that makes you wanna grab a partner and start swinging your hips. *"Oye como va... benito...bueno...como sa!"*

I sit there staring at that house, that house of blood. And then...I'm not dead anymore. My maternal instincts have kicked into high gear, and busted that zombie shell wide open. And I have geared up and suited up in my maternal suit of armor. My mind is made up! I will puke, crap and die and see my Jesus, before I set foot out of this cab. I'm ready now, I'm ready to fight like a bear for her cubs...I'm ready to fight like a mother for her child. So let Miss Selma bring it on. Because I'm sho-nuf ready to get it on!

Mama slides out of the cab first. I can't move...I won't move. It's as if my clothes have been stapled to that car seat. "Annie Mae, get yo ass outta that car...NOW," she orders. And I look at that woman as if she lost what little mind she ever had. And still I won't move. And still I don't move.

Then Mama reaches in and pulls and jerks on my arm like it's a damn slot machine. I grip that shiny door handle on the other side. And I'm ready to rock steady! I have no intention of leaving this car. I wouldn't leave this car if Ed frigging McMahon had popped in front of my face, waving a check from the Publisher's Clearing House. Mama nods her head and says, "So that's how ya wanna play it, huh?" She twists her mouth, and adds a "Hmmmm…hmm." And I roll my eyes, with yellow lights of caution blinking in front of me.

Then the cab driver turns around and gives me the evil eye. And he's a big bruiser, looking something, with bushy eyebrows, bushy mustache and even bushier hair, that stands at attention on the top of his head. He's making Don King look like a poster-child for Vidal Sassoon. And he looks to me like he's put one too many ghetto whippings on somebody's body. He continues to look at me, so I suck my teeth, fold my arms, and give him eye for eye, and look for look.

"Hey," Mama yells to the cab driver, shoving a bill in his face, "I'll give you $50.00 if you help me get my daughter outta yo cab."

"Sure, sure!" he says, in a heavy Polish accent, already stuffing the money into his shirt pocket. Bruiser gets out of that cab and comes around to the open side, and I swear up and down that man towers over that car like King Kong to a bus stop.

He takes his beefy hands that are the size of dinner plates, and lunges them into the open door. I scoot to the far side of the cab and I hail screams and feet into his chest. I get a good grip on my friend, the door handle. And I let my feet do the talking.

The Bruiser is getting really mad now. He's muttering something in Polish, underneath his breath, and smacking his fist into his other hand. And he pokes his head inside of the cab again, and he clamps those whopper hands down on my face and neck…What did he do that for? My teeth sink down into that man's hands like I'm having a Big Mac Attack.

Bruiser snatches back his bleeding hand and hisses, "Yooou Bitch," with hate and venom dripping out of every letter. Now God knows, that I didn't harbor an ounce of hate for this man, I'm just trying to protect what's mine, that's all. Now, isn't that the way of a mother? Isn't that what any mother would do for her child?

And I'm trying my best to watch those beefy hands, while scrambling to open the nearest door. And before I can say, Jack Johnson, Bruiser hauls off and rams his fist into my face. I roll over and a flash bulb of pain flicks before my eyes. And I lie there, on the floor of the cab, not moving, afraid of breathing, asking myself for the umpteenth time…why. Why would Mama allow this man to beat on me like this, because regardless of my crimes, my blood is HER blood. Regardless, if I'm as wrong as a serial killer…her bone is MY bone.

He grabs me by my defeated legs and yanks me out of the cab. My dress scoots up in the back and my behind and back side scrapes against the rough floor of the cab. I'm afraid of this man now. I'm afraid that if I fight him anymore, make the slightest move anymore, that he'll hurt me. Bruiser will mess my face up so bad that next to me, the Elephant Man will look like Miss Diana Ross'. Now, I've never been what you would call pretty, but my eyes and nose are in the right place and I intend to keep it that way.

As Bruiser pulls me to my feet, the evening breeze whips across my sore legs and face. And my legs feel all wobbly, like I've gone through a medieval torture chamber. Bruiser spots my mother coming down the stairs of the frame house, and he gets the Quasimodo grin on his face, and yanks me up proudly by the collar, like he's posing for the cover of Field & Stream Magazine.

There's a Hispanic man with Mama. That man…that man, he has the body of a matador, with long, dark hair that drapes across his shoulders. And those eyes…oh those eyes…Lord have mercy that man sent feelings shooting through me that the nuns in grade school told me were a mortal sin. I feel like I should rush home and beat myself down, with a belt soaked in Holy Water. That man has honey liquid eyes, honey liquid eyes…you could get lost up in those eyes. You would be gone for so long they would have to send out a search party. There's a steamy sexuality that pops off this man, like water from a greasy skillet (PING…PING…PING)!

He looks at me now, and those honey liquid eyes crinkle up and smile. And I turn my head away, afraid he might read my feelings. As he comes closer, he says, "Don't be afraid, Chiquita. In my village in Med-hi-co, I perform this procedure meanie, meanie times." That accent…oh that accent, it's as fluid as a drop of rain.

And then for a wisp of a moment, the abortion doesn't exist. The Bruiser doesn't exist. My mother doesn't exist. The only thing that exists is him, me, and that accent. We exist in a world of smoke and shadows. I want him to touch me now. I want him to touch my hair, my face, my neck…my pain.

And he reaches out to touch my hand. And I reach out to touch his hand. His hand comes closer and my hand comes closer…he touches me…and…I jerk my hand away! I jerk my hand away, as hard as I can. And I wipe it on my dress as hard as I can, with a scowl on my face. It's something about that man's hands.

There was something downright disgusting in that man's hands. Almost as if he's hiding a dirty little secret, just beneath his calluses. And I search his eyes again for a hint of that dirty little secret. But the only thing I see is that honey liquid begging me to dab up a taste.

Bruiser's tug and yank on my collar whips me back to the folds of reality. I look at Mama, with pleading eyes and I scream into her face, "Why Mama, why?"

Why was she allowing me to be treated this way? I remember, growing up, if I went home crying about a big bully, that had attacked me, Mama would stomp hell fire up to the parents' door. She would make it clear that, if they didn't take care of their child, she would take care of them. And what she couldn't do, she'd pay someone to do. Needless to say, that the next day in school was as cool as an igloo. That's why it's so hard for me to understand her complete about face.

Mama cuts her eyes at the Meat Grinder. The Meat Grinder cuts his eyes at Mama. And Mama slowly nods her head. At her signal, the Meat Grinder pulls a syringe from his pants pocket, a long syringe of a thing, glowing under the street lights. At the sight of it, I start squirming and wiggling, like a fish out of water. Then the Meat Grinder grabs my arm and I'm really screaming and a tussling now. And the funny thing about it is that while I'm throwing out hell on a thunderbolt, nobody but nobody out on the block seems to be paying me any mind. It's as if I'm invisible or something. The little girls go on playing double Dutch; the little boys go on playing stick ball. The teenagers go on drinking wine, smoking weed, and weaving dreams.

"1…2…3…4, who's come a knocking at my door," the little girls play into the jump rope.

"Foul ball…foul ball," the little boys scream into the Louisville Slugger.

"S i i i p….Mane, I'm gonna make me some tall cash," says the teen inhaling his dreams. And the fire hydrant roars and flushes their dreams back down into the sewer.

And Mama, Mama stands there, watching me, without watching me, seeing me, without seeing me. Saying chucks of nothing and doing chucks of nothing…Whipping my behind without laying a finger on my behind. You see, I had forgotten, that Mama's umbilical cord has turned into an invisible strap. A strap that she carries with her at all times, in her purse, bra, or sometimes, in her pantyhose. And she's always ready to whip that strap out anytime, and any place. She waves it in my face, to remind me that she's running this circus.

Mama still stands there, with a silent slit for a mouth and clumps of coal for eyes. She's looking right at me, but not seeing me. She's gone someplace else, a place where I'm not allowed to follow.

"Mama....Mama," I scream into her empty face. "MAMA!" My voice echoes across the houses, bounces across the light poles and drops dead on the pavement.

With glaring eyes the Meat Grinder pulls off the cap of the syringe with his teeth. He holds it up to the moonlight and pushes the plunger. Drops of liquid shoot through the air, like fireworks.

Upon seeing this, I'm squirming and wiggling, and doing a voodoo dance. And the only place I can go is down...down. And I start sinking, like the good ship Titanic. And then I notice Bruiser's fat toes winking at me from his sandals.

And....BASH! I stomp those suckers, like water bugs. He lets go of my collar, and grabs his foot with a were-wolf's howl, "AAHOOOOHHHH!"

And I take off, like a Lear Jet down the street, weaving and bobbing past the girls playing double Dutch. I zig and zag through the boys playing stick ball. And I jack and knife around the corner. I notice a wall just then, a brick wall. And there's a glowing sign in the middle that reads, "DEAD END." I turn to one side and it's blocked off. On the other side there's a tall, chain-link fence, with a row of mean looking spikes at the top, and there's and empty lot behind it.

Now, I've never been much on the tom-boy side's I never climbed a tree or a fence. But I step back from that fence now, and I spit on my hands and rub them together. Because ain't nothing to it, but to go on and do it. So I fit my hand into one loop and my feet into the other. And with every movement the fence clangs and shakes a little. As I go up higher I can feel my breast and my stomach pressing against the loops, and after every step I look back to see if I see Mama or her flunkies charging.

As I come to the top I make sure that my fingers curb the loops of the fence and not the spikes at the top. And as I hoist my leg onto the other side, freedom whispers in my ear, "You're almost there now. On the other side, there's a new life for you and your baby. Climb it...climb it...and don't look back." And....

"Get your nasty hands off me!" I can feel him before I can see him.

The Meat Grinder yanks at my leg, trying to pull me down. And the spikes yank into my inner thighs. "Chiquita, come down now, what chew are doing is very, very dangerous," he says.

I straddle the fence and say, "What YOU"RE planning on doing is very, very dangerous."

I hear the click of Mama's heels, echoing across the alley bricks. "Annie Mae, get yo crazy ass down from there," she orders, stomping her feet and flaring her nostrils.

"Naw, Mama, I ain't coming down. Do you hear me! I ain't coming down. All my life, Mama, I done what you wanted me to do. and I've been what you wanted me to be, but it stops tonight Mama, right here…right now, it stops!" I say, shaking and clanging my feet against the fence. I look up at he silver moon and I wish I could just reach out and grab it. And let it satellite my dreams and my tomorrows. "I ain't never wanted to be no opera singer, Mama. That was your dream, not mine. My dreams lie on the other side of this fence. And I intend to find them. Do you hear me Mama; I'm going to find my own dreams. And live my own life. My own life! I can't live yours anymore….I just can't," I scream, and at that moment, all of the hurt and all of the pain of a life time, digs and tears into my thighs.

Mama looks up at me, and she lets go of a long, hard sigh, and says to the Meat Grinder, "Do what ya gotta do." She cuts her eyes at me one last time and turns and walks away. Only this time there isn't any pep in Mama's step or glide in her stride. She walks away with slumped shoulders, as if she's weighted down by a back-pack, a back-pack of guilt.

The Meat Grinder slams my foot into the fence and the vibrating echo calls out my mother's name. I look down at him and I see it then. All that honey liquid masking tape has been peeled away, and I see him for the true demon he is. I'm trying my best to twist and turn to get my leg loose, but the more I twist and turn, the deeper the spikes go into my thighs. "Why don't you leave me alone," I beg. "Please leave me alone. Just tell her that I got away, that's all, she won't know…You're hurting me…you're hurting me so bad!"

"Oh, but I will know Chiquita, I will know. And chew are only hurting yourself. Your mamasita loves chew very, very much. She only wants the best for chew," he says aiming my foot towards the street light. Then, he narrows his eyes and glides his finger, from my ankle to my toes and then back up again. And he stops half way up, and starts slapping my foot, like a new born baby…WHOP… WHOP…WHOP. And I'm getting scared now, and I'm twisting and turning. My thighs feel like they're being cut open by hot razor blades. And his fingers…his fingers are like a nest of snakes coiling and uncoiling around my foot. "Somebody help me," I scream up at the moon. But there's nobody there, but the darkness, the Meat Grinder, and my dying dream. Sometimes I wonder, was God even there?

He jabs that needle into my foot, now. And my veins crackle and burn, like a forest fire. "Nawww…..Nawwwww," I whisper, shaking my head. And I pull and I jerk and I……..and the banging of the fence vibrates the word: failure…failure. And I fall; I fall into a funnel of darkness.

"Mommy can't catch me," he laughs, as he does his little tetter-totter bow-legged run. He throws back his head and laughs,and his baby teeth glimmer against the sunlight. He's two years old now, and we're running in a field of lilacs and daffodils.

"I'm coming to get yooooou," I say playfully, running behind him, with my arms stretching out. And then he disappears into a tall thicket of grass. "Antwon, where are you. Mommy is going to get yooooou." And his childish giggles float through the air.

BOOM…BOOM…BOOM…BOOM. "Antwon!" I say, raising my voice a notch, trying to mask my fear. But I can't hear anything, but a banging drum. "Antwon!" I scream. I don't hear his laughter anymore. And I'm running up the hill, calling out his name. BOOM…BOOM…BOOM…BOOM. I cover my ears because the sound is getting louder and louder…BOOM…BOOM…BOOM! And the lilacs and the daffodils turn into a landslide of brown gook. And I see it coming, and I try to run. But my feet get caught in this brown gook. I try to lift one foot and then the other, but they're sinking farther and farther down, like they're weighted down with cinder blocks. And something is tugging at my legs something from underneath, trying to pull me down with it. Then for a moment everything is still. I hear birds chirping in a distance.

I look down at the brown gook and it starts to bubbling and gurgling. And it's Mama! She jumps up from that brown gook. SPLASH! And she's been drenched in that gook. But her eyes…her eyes, burn through me, like acid. "ANTWON!" I scream, looking around in a panic and stepping back. "ANTWON!" Mama grabs me with her murky looking arms and tries to pull me under! My hands flap and lick at the gook. SPLASH…SPLASH…SPLASH! She straddles my shoulders and clamps down on my mouth and nose and pushes me under…pushes me under! BOOM…BOOM…BOO…

When I awaken it's as if a gauze bandage is unraveling from my eyes. And I can hear the swishing and splashing of water. I blink a couple of times, and then I can make out the figure of the Meat Grinder. His hair is tied back in a pony tail. And he's washing his hands in an old fashioned tin basin, with a red rim around it. I look around and I notice an old fashioned kitchen sink full of dishes and rust stains, with a ruffled flowery skirt at the bottom. And there's an empty chair in the corner, where Mama should have been. I'm lying on a sticky pile of green garbage bags on top of a kitchen table. He raises his head and arches an eyebrow, when he notes that I'm awake.

And the smell of fresh blood bear hugs the walls, the ceiling, and the floor…my blood. He continues to wash his hands in the bloody, pink water…my baby's blood. And I look down past my knees, and I see…the baby…my baby. With a chocolate face…my face. His little thumb is in his little mouth…my thumb…my mouth.

And Lord, Lord, Lord, I tell you, I scream. A scream that starts at the bottom of my empty womb, rushes past my throat and leaps outta my mouth. I scream out the frigging injustice of it all. I scream so loud that they can hear me on the stair steps to the Supreme Court. I scream so loud it makes Rowe vs. Wade look like a damn fairy tale. I scream so loud it can resurrect an army of babies. I scream so loud…I scream so loud…I scream …loud…but my baby is gone, gone, gone, and ain't nothing going to bring him back. And tears run down my cheeks. And the pain runs through my stomach, and empty, empty pain.

And through the curtain of my tears, I see the Meat Grinder's smiling face. And I want to leap from that table and slap that bastard back up his mama's birth canal! He knew what he was doing. He wanted me to see my baby. He wanted to see my pain…my suffering.

And then without tearing those honey liquid eyes from mine, he scoops my stone dead baby into the palm of his hand and tosses it into the garbage can…the garbage can, way on the other side of the room. And the little brown baby spins across the room in a death spiral and his little brown body twists and turns…turns and twists. Spinning…spinning…spinning. And then for a whisper of a second it seems as if I can see, the whites of my baby's eyes, floating around and around. Now you can call me dumb, stupid, or just plain outta my mind crazy. But I know what I saw, I know what I saw! Then his little brown body turns upside down, like a salt shaker, going head first, tumbling, and tumbling, down, down, down, into the garbage can. "BOOMBOOMBOOMBOOM." And upon impact the garbage can tilts and twirls, twirls and tilts, threatening to spill over…and then it stands still…cradling my baby. And the plastic inside of the can slides farther down with a crinkling moan….a grave….my baby's grave.

Then the Meat Grinder jerks my arm and stabs me with another needle. And he puts his face right down into my face, his breath right down into my breath, his pores right down into my pores, his blood thread eyes, right down into my blood thread eyes. And then he says, "Good night….Puta." And he takes his tongue and laps it across my face.

BAM….I awaken that night, in my bed, with a pounding pain, punching its way out of my stomach. BAM…BAM! I curl up and try to rock away the pain. Then, I feel something, something hot and sticky rolling down my legs….an apple of blood. And it's followed by a geyser of blood. I want to get out of bed, but I'm too weak to get out of bed. But I want to hold on to life too much to stay there and drown in that bed. Maybe Mama was right there could be more babies in my future, after I had a career and settled down and got married. But right now, the chance of grabbing hold of my future was like grabbing hold of water with my bare hands. Tears of sweat pop off of my forehead and drop down my wet bosom. I roll over to the edge of the mattress and I roll out. And the side of my hip hits the coolness of the floor…POW! And I crawl; I crawl out of the room, leaving behind a trail of blood and a trail of fear.

As I crawl into my mother's room, I know that the Grim Reaper is waiting for me, in the dark, in the corner. He's waiting there, with his dark heavy robes spilling across the floor like hot tar. He's waiting for me to stop, waiting for my last strand of hope to slither away. So he can float across the floor boards and touch me with his spidery, gray fingers. He's waiting to vampire the life out of me…waiting.

My every step, my every movement, seems as if I'm being weighted down, weighted down by dropping stones, another and another. I can't see nothing but a pool of darkness that's threatening to open its mouth and swallow me whole. I try to squint my eyes and shake it off, squint my eyes and crawl it off.

When I reach my mother's room, I feel around for her bed. I tug at her feet. She kicks at her sheets, and rolls over with a grunt. I take in a dry gulp of regret, and I tug at her feet again....nothing. I try to call out her name, I open my mouth....nothing. I can feel sour bile rising in my throat. I swallow it back down. And I make my way to the head of the bed. I tap her lightly on the shoulder. I want to give her a yank and a jerk, but I'm oh-so weak. My white gown hangs heavy and wet with blood. Again I open my mouth to call out her name. And with great effort my throat squeezes out a whispered, "Maaaa....Maaaa," I say, tapping her on the shoulder again.

Mama opens her eyes just then, squinting and blinking her way through the darkness. "Annie Mae?" she asks. I let go of a heavy sigh, and plop my head upon her sheets and I give in to the darkness.

When I flutter my eyes open, I'm surrounded by a bleached whiteness. And there's a woman floating towards me with what at first looks like a white gown and a blue halo. But as I look closer, I see that it's a lab coat and a puffy surgical bonnet with blonde curls dipping and dabbing against her forehead, and a pair of friendly wire frames surrounding her eyes.

"Hi, Sweet Pea," she says as she cups my hand and scoots up a chair with the other. And a mournful sound screeches across the floor. "I'm Dr. Greenblatt. You've had a rough go of it, huh?" I nod my head and tears of self pity stand ready at the back of my lashes. "Yeah, I know, Hon....I know," she says stroking my hands. Her warm smooth hands are like a healing balm that seems to lick away at the corners of my pain.

"Well," she says, taking in a big gulp of hesitation, "everything is fine now. You lost a great deal of blood. It was really touch and go there for awhile. We were worried about you, Sweet Pea, we didn't want to lose you. And we gave you a tetanus shot and some minor stitching for your legs. You were pretty torn up down there. You want to tell me what hap..." The look in my eyes tells her all she needs to know. She twists her mouth and nods her head. "I understand, Sweet Pea...I understand," she says.

She searches the walls and the floor for something she can't seem to find. And she grips my hand, she grips my hand so hard her knuckles go from pink to white. "Your uterus was completely ruptured from the abortion," she chokes, "And we had to remove it. I'm afraid that you'll never have any more children."

And my mouth forms a perfect "O". As if she had balled up all of my pain and all of my shock and stuffed it into my mouth. "I'm sorry, Sweet Pea. I'm so, so sorry," she whispers. And the tears and the pain roll from my eyes. Dr. Greenblatt grabs me by my shoulders and pulls me towards her. Her lab coat smells of iodine and Phisoderm Soap. "That's right, Sweet Pea," she says, "Cry if it makes you feel better. Cry until your well runs dry. Just cry, Sweet Pea…just cry." And I let go, I let go of all the tears, all the hurt. I let them grow and swell into her lab coat, like a festering germ. And she rocks me…back…and forward…and she holds me…back…and forward, for what seems like a long, long time.

Mama swings my room door open a few hours later, carrying loads upon loads of yellow roses. She knows they're my favorite. She catches a breath and says in a teasing voice. "Girl, you look like the picture of health. Get yo ass up outta that bed."

She prances over towards me. "Look what I got for ya. It'll add some color to your room," she says, dumping them at the foot of my bed searching underneath the cabinet sink for a vase. She pulls out a big green one. "This one heah will do just fine," she says. Mama goes about her business of humming a little happy tune, and overstuffing the flowers in the vase. She places the vase on the window sill and continues to arrange them, "Well, what ya think, Annie Mae," she asks, stepping back from her creation and rubbing her hands on her hips.

I turn over in bed, facing her and say, "I think you're trying to kill me…that's what I think."

"What the hell are you talking about?" she asks, bristling up her anger, ready to attack.

"You know what I'm talking about," I say, raising myself out of bed. "Because of you and that botched abortion, I'll never have a child of my own…Because of YOU….YOU!" I scream, pounding my fist on the mattress.

Mama, slinks towards me like a panther, "Because of me," she asks, pointing her finger to her chest, "Because of me!…Bitch, I ain't never told you to go out there and gap yo legs open for some half-breed Mother Fucker…How ya think I feel sitting up there, in that kitchen, watching that man pull that half-breeds shit outta yo ass? Bitch, I had to get up off my ass and run outside. I had to bust open that damn door!...But ta show you what yo hot-in-the-ass ways had cost, I told that man to leave that dead baby right there, and let you see it…let you look down, and see yo own sin! The way I had ta look down and see it…Hmmm….Hmm." Mama starts pacing the floor, back and forth, forth and back. And the click of her heels against the tile seems to hammer in my pain and her words, deeper and deeper. POW…POW…POW!

"Hmmm….Hmmmm," she says, fingering her watch and her rings. "Hmmmm….Hmmmm ….The Lord talked to me, night before last, Annie Mae. Hmmmm….Hmmmm….I asked him to show me the way, and He did. Hmmmm…Hmmmmm….He told me….He told me, that I had invested too much time, money, and hope into your future….Hmmmmm….Hmmmmmm," she says, still pacing, still fingering her watch and her rings, "to let you, or any half-breed Motha Fucka come along and fuck it up. So I fixed yo ass,I fixed yo ass,Bitch! Like a goddamn cat in heat!...Hmmm….Hmmmm. Yes I did it!" she says as she paces towards the window sill. She claws her hands on the edge of the window and haunches her back up and sips in a breath so hard that for a moment, only a moment, it looks as if a giant stump is hanging beneath her clothing. And then she lets go of the breath and her back smoothes out again. And Mama throws back her head and proclaims, "Yes I did it goddammit….and I'd do it again!"

Part VI

Circa 1976

It happened! Just the way Mama said it would happen. Julliard asks me to come and audition….ME! After they listen to my tape that I sent them, they want to hear and see me….Annie Mae Jenkins! Me, Annie Mae, who's closest friend is a record player and the glare of the T.V. screen. Me….Annie Mae who gets pinned more jokes on than a tail on a donkey—Ooh! I tell you, I'm as happy as a starving man munching on a pork chop! Me and Mama are on our way to the Grande Apple!

That hot August evening after the audition me and Mama go to see a Broadway show, *THE WIZ*, And we go out to dinner afterwards. At the restaurant she has a couple of whiskey sours. And she even lets me have a couple glasses of white wine, which I know as much about as a dog knows about Sunday school. Ooh, but I know one thing; it tastes awfully good with my Greek Chicken.

So by the time me and Mama get back to the hotel room, I'm as high as a Georgia pine. Mama slides her key into the door and what do I see, but a long brown bottle of Long Island Iced Tea on the table next to the window, with a set of glasses. I freeze in the doorway. And I look at the bottle and I look at Mama, because you see, Mama ain't never been too much of a liquor sipper. "Don't just stand there in the door way looking like a statute. Go on down the hall and get some ice. Hell, we're gonna celebrate tonight." Mama says, shoving the silver ice bucket in my face. "My baby is going to Julliard hmmp…hmmp…hmmp," Mama says, dancing and a prancing through the room, justa swinging her hips, making her way to the table with the liquor glasses on it.

"What demon got into YOU tonight? You ain't never even let me look at a drink, let alone taste one," I say, setting the now full ice bucket down on the table.

"Baby, I'm as happy as a sissy with a banana in his mouth," Mama says, having a sit down. She had cut the radio on while I was gone. And the sound of a mournful Teddy Peddygrass fills the air. "Besides you're eighteen now, Baby. And there are three things in life you must learn how ta handle, and that's yo man, yo money, and yo liquor," she says, while pouring the drinks over the popping ice.

I scoot up a chair, with a twist to my mouth, and a frown in my brow. And Mama cocks her head to ask, "What you looking all grumpy for? This is YO day Baby, shouldn't nothing be bringing you down."

I smack on my tongue and say, "Mama do really think I'll be accepted at Julliard?"

And Mama looks over at me with a smile to her lips and says, "Naww baby, I don't think you'll be accepted at Julliard. I KNOW you will Baby! As sure as I KNOW I wanna see my Jesus. Now sit yo behind down here, and enjoy yourself."

I get real comfortable in that chair then ,and I notice that the lamp light leaves a soft-brown tinge on Mama's face, a tinge that takes away her threads of hardness and leaves something soft and girlish there instead. I take a healthy swig of my drink, and I smack my lips several times and say, "It taste like brown Kool-Aid Mama."

Mama leans her head over her drink and says, "Well, that's one Kool-Aid that will knock ya on yo ass. You better take it easy with that stuff. And I bite down on my lip, and I stare at Mama's nearly empty glass. And you see, for the first time and only time, I feel so close to that woman on the other side of the table. You see, she isn't my Mama anymore she's my friend. And I realize how good and relax I feel with Mama. I think back on all the fun we had together all day, auditioning at Julliard, going to the theater together, and dining together. I couldn't count all the times that day we had thrown back our heads and laughed together. And riding on the railroads of my memory, I can't ever remember having so much fun with my Mama, not even as a child. I just can't remember.

And then I feel a burning in my stomach. Now to this day I don't know if it's the alcohol or just the plain excitement of the day. But the burning is niggling at me…see? And it's telling me I can do or say whatever I want to. Now, I try to fold up this feeling, and tuck it away somewhere. But ooh, I tell you, it's burning a hole of confidence into my belly. A confidence I ain't never had before, especially around Mama.

"Annie Mae!" Mama shouts, "I don't know where yo mind is, but ya better find it." Mama looks at me with an under eyed smile, clinks the ice around in her now empty glass and says, "Aren't you gonna pour your mama another drink?"

"Oh, okay Mama," I say pouring the liquor over the crackling ice. And before I know it, that burning confidence is putting words into my mouth. "You know Mama," I say, still pouring the drinks into the glasses, "You know Mama, you ain't never told me how it was before I was born, with you, Daddy and Gloria. Were things different back then," I ask, watching her from the corner of my eye.

Mama picks up her drink and rolls it across the side of her face. And with narrow eyes and puckered lips she draws in a reluctant breath and says, "Now you know, I ain't never been one ta talk too much about the past. I'm one to talk about tomorrow, and the day after that. That's how I got you this Julliard audition…by looking forward Annie Mae, not behind me. The past is for the dead and the dying Baby. And I'd rather leave it that way."

And my fingers press against the edge of the table. And my curiosity presses against the edge of the table. And my face presses closer to her's. And that burning confidence presses against the edge of my lips, and says, "I appreciate everything you've done for me Mama. And I know that if it wasn't for you, I wouldn't have gotten this audition. But don't you think that I have a right to know Mama? You're a part of me and I'm a part of you. So anyway you look at it, the past has quilted us both together. Your past is MY past Mama, and you can't change that."

Mama's eyes travel to the ceiling light. And they stay there for a long, long time. And then she slowly glides her hand across the side of her face, as if she's trying to pull out the truth. And it's as if the truth gets stuck in her throat, because Mama takes in a long swig of her drink. And she slides the drink across the table. And the sound of the ice clinking against the glass races through the room. And I look up at the small ceiling chandelier and it seems to tingle and sway.

And Mama opens up her mouth, and opens up a room of truth. A room I have never seen before. And there are dark things in that room. Things that have been hidden for so long that they're full of dust and cobwebs. Things that her and Daddy kept buried in a cavern of secrets.

Like soon after they were married they get a visit from the white horse (heroin). And they have to separate for awhile. Because Daddy gets so strung out on that little teaspoon of white nothing, he's taking and stealing everything he can from Mama…and that's including her dignity. And Mama is setting out more truths on that table, than the Pope sets out blessings. And sitting back in that chair listening to Mama, something hits me. It hits me like a bag of quarters, that I ain't just pouring drinks into Mama's glass. I'm pouring her a truth cocktail. Because the drink goes in, and shonuf, truth spills out!

Mama takes another long gulp on that truth cocktail. And I watch her dark brown throat muscles go up, down, down and up again. And she sets the glass down with a slight thump and both of her hands hold on tightly to that glass, like she's holding on to a prayer. She hears an old Sam Cooke record on the radio. She rocks back and forward, and she sings along with the record, *"I was born by the river in a little tent. And ooh, just like the river I've been running every since.*," and Mama nods her head and bites down on her lips a little bit.

Mama slouches back in the chair, and says, "In the mid fifties, it was kinda hard being a single parent in a big city, 'specially one with no damn job. And I remember this one day; the damn sun is doing a heat dance on my back. It's a hotter than hot day in July. I've been sweating, praying and a cursing all morning long for a job. My old laundry job where me and yo Daddy usta work, had let me go. I guess they figure whatever kinda drugs he's doing, I'm probably doing them too. Well, anyway I have been pounding on that pavement so hard looking for a job, my damn heel breaks. So Lord, Lord, I'm justa hopping and a limping…limping and a hopping. And I make it to the corner of Clybourn and Vine. And I notice this little bar sitting on the corner called the Kotton Klub. And it's spelled with a "K". Now, ain't that cute?" Mama says, justa grinning. "And there's about seven, half circle, stone steps leading up to the bar. And the door is wide open. I tell ya, it looks so dark, and cool up in there. And I look up at the ceiling, and I see this big ole ceiling fan, with these big, dusty blades, going round and around…WHOMP…WHOMP… WHOMP. Its justa spreading that cool air like an angel spreads her wings. I can almost feel that coolness from the outside."

"Child, look like that cool air was calling my name. And I know good and well I can't afford to go up in there. I can't afford nothing but the Grace of God. Well, before I know it, I zoom up those steps. And I plop my burden and behind down on the barstool."

"And at first, I don't see nobody's body. And it's dark up in there Annie Mae, except for a few scattered neon beer signs. And there's a small naked light bulb that sits on the top of the middle wall. And that little light sure does its job, justa bouncing pretty colors off of the brown, green and clear liquor bottles that sit beneath it, in front of a long, dusty mirror, but otherwise, it s pitch-black in there."

"And something tells me ta look in the corner, way off to the other side of the bar. And I see this shot glass hanging in mid-air, with this white rag going in and out, and around and around, and in that glass again. Child, I'm ready now, I'm ready ta give my soul to Jesus and my ass to the undertaker. I just KNOW I'm looking at a haint (a ghost). And then the haint speaks, and says, "May I help you?" Child, I'm ready ta jump up outta that chair and start swinging from that ceiling fan. And the voice comes closer, "May I help you," it says for the second time. That's when I notice that it's just a man, but you see Baby, this ain't just any man. This man is BLACK. And I ain't talking about that smooth, pretty black….this man is crusty black. Child look like you can take a knife, and scrape that black right off of ‘em, like burnt on toast."

"And Annie Mae ta make matters worse, he's only got one eye…one eye. And it's always leaking or pusing at the sides. And he's justa standing there, dressed in all black, justa sucking on a tooth pick. Child, Child, Child, you wanna talk about ugly? Man is so ugly he can turn his mama's breast milk into feta cheese!" she says, throwing back her curls, justa laughing, and slamming her hand down on the table.

Mama cuts the laughter short, and looks long and hard at the table lamp. And the lamp light sits on her face like a yellow mask. "But ya know what Annie Mae, that ugly man sucking on that tooth pick, looks at me with that one eye, and I know he has sized me up in the time it takes to light a match. And I tell ya, it's scary Annie Mae. To see him justa standing there, pushing and sucking on that tooth-pick, and justa nodding his head, like he's letting you know, he KNOWS all yo little back-door secrets."

"He cast that one eye on me, and for the third time says, "May I help YOU?"

Now, I ain't got enough money in my pocket ta buy a piece of lint. But I'm so hot and thirsty; I don't know what else ta do. So with a nervous nod and a smile I say, "How much is a Coke?"

"25 cents," he says.

"So I fish around in my purse, and I search around in there, and I think I have three cents to my name. And Baby, I'm so afraid that he's gonna kick me to the curb. But Mr. Hunt, that's his name, waves his hand and smacks his teeth, and says, "That's alright, it's on me." And I let go of a long, grateful sigh. But I'm still nervous because you can't go around expecting something for nothing. And I guess I kinda give him a cock-eyed look. And he says, "Don't worry about it Miss Lady, I ain't out for nothing. You just seem kinda thirsty, that's all." He starts scanning me with that one eye again, and pushing around that tooth-pick, and ask, "Ya looking for a job ain't ya," sliding that Coke over to me. "Judging by the way you're all dressed up in yo Sunday finery, and here it is Monday and all." I nod my head real fast, and start sipping on that Coke. "You seem like a nice settled lady. I been looking for someone ta help me out around heah." Now, I look around in that bar and I don't see nobody, but me, him and the dust mites.

And there ain't a 'HELP WANTED' sign nowhere to be found. And he says, "Oh, I know it ain't crowded now, but gets on later in the evening, it gets pretty crowded up in heah."

"I don't know," I say, shaking my head. "I'm trying to finish my drink so I can get the hell up outta there. I ain't use ta nobody offering me something off the bat. I'm thinking he wants ta pull a few rabbits outta my hat. But I ain't gonna let 'em."

He throws his hands up in the air and says, "Wait a minute Miss Lady. Hold on there now. I ain't after no fun and games, if that's what ya thinking. When I was 8 years old down in Natchez, Mississippi I traded in my play toys for the back of a mule and a plow. And I ain't played a game or picked up a playing card since. So if I can't come to ya real Miss Lady, I ain't coming to ya at all. You just seem like a mighty nice lady, in need of help that's all. I ain't trying ta take advantage of you or nothing. I just wanna help ya. And looking at yo shoes when ya first walked up in heah, and the few cents in yo pocket book, you can use a little help…can't ya?" he says, justa sucking on that tooth-pick, and justa rolling it from one side of his mouth to the other."

"And I cast my eyes to my lap in shame, Annie Mae. A shame that burns from the back of my neck to the heels of my feet, and I just wanna run up outta there. But that shame is like a can of Crisco, it just slides me farther, and farther down in my seat. He smacks his lips then, and pushes that tooth-pick to the other side of his mouth, and says, "What ya sitting there with yo head hung down for Miss Lady? Hold yo head up, you ain't killed nobody. And you sure ain't got nothing to be ashamed of. Life ain't nothing but an elevator ride Miss Lady, sometimes you go up, and sometimes you go down. But if you're real unlucky, you get stuck between floors, and can't go nowhere at all."

"Then he scans me with that one eye again and says, "Ya don't look like ya got any kids, but going by that worried look on yo face, I'd say, ya got at least one mouth ta feed…am I right? And you're from down home ain't ya? You don't look slickified like these other Marys and Janes that come flouncing their behinds up in heah."

"And Annie Mae, I just nod my head. And I'm about ready to hit the pavement. I'm tired of this ugmo asking me all of these questions, like he's a goddamn game show host. Questions he SEEMS ta know all the answers to.

And it's the funniest thang. I'll never forget it. Just as I twist the barstool around, I'm still holding my glass of Coke, with this paper straw in it. And I'm justa sloshing, raking around in the ice, searching for that last good corner. And I'm justa slurping and a gurgling on that last little bit, at the bottom of the glass. Hell, it's good ta me. And I don't wanna give it up. And I look outside that open door, at that wide, gray pavement, with the hot, afternoon sun, justa streaking down on it. And Lord, Lord, Lord, what do I see, coming along, but this young, black mother about my age. And she's justa raggedy. She's wearing an ole dirty, cotton slip, trying to pass it off as a dress. Her hair is all kinky, look like it ain't seen a brush or a comb in days. And look like she's fallen down in some mud or something, 'cause the back of her legs are caked with it. And Baby, on top of all that, she has three stair step children, and by the swell of her belly, look like she might be 'specting another, and she's got one in her arms, and two at her sides. And all three kids ain't wearing nothing but saggy diapers on their behinds. And the oldest one, he ain't no more than two and a half, or three, pulls on her dress tail. His little nose is justa snotty, and he says, "Mama I'm hungry, I'm so hungry Mama.'' And he's justa crying and pulling on her dress tail. "Hush now, hush…Mama's gonna figure out something," she says, rubbing the little boy's head. And that po woman stops palming that child's head, and she looks straight up at me, and I look straight down at her. And for a moment look like nothing else exist in this whole wide WORLD, but me and that woman, looking eye ta eye, and feeling pain for pain. And Lord, her face looks so much like my face.

It's like looking at words in a mirror. And the words are just alike, but they come out backwards."

"And it hits me Annie Mae…It hits me like a fucking Mack Truck… I ain't been sipping on no Coke, I've been drinking down a cold glass of fear. A fear that slides across my tongue, down my throat, and it hugs the curves and the grooves of my stomach…FEAR.

And I'm so afraid Annie Mae…I'm so afraid of becoming that woman. I'm afraid that if I get up and walk outta this bar right now, that her fate will become my fate. Lord I just hope and pray that at her journey's end that she finds a cool drink of water and a heaping bowl of comfort. God bless her…God bless her."

"That lady and her kids move on, but my fear doesn't. It has me duct taped to that bar stool." Mama's fingers skates across the table, making invisible figure eights, all around the sides, and up towards the middle, and she says, "And I look over at this one eyed man, named Mr. Leroi Hunt. And I stare deep and hard at that one eye. And I look beneath that yellowish film, and the crusty corner of that one eye, and I see something, Annie Mae. I see the truth, and it's right there, justa smiling."

"Now, I don't know for sure what this ugmo man has ta offer me…but I know it's a piece of something." And then Mama wags her finger and her head and says, "Because ya see Annie Mae, a bird in the hand is better than a thousand in the bush. So I didn't get up from that seat. I bite down on my pride and my suspicion, and I stay Annie Mae, I stay with that little black bird, that's holding a little worm in his mouth. That little black bird called Mr. Leroi Hunt. And I take that little worm, and that little piece of something." And Mama lifts up her eyes, and looks out the window, way above the towering sky line and she watches the blinking lights of a plane passing by, and says, "And I ain't never looked back."

Mama cocks her head, and looks at me all funny like, "What's wrong Mama," I ask.

"Child please," Mama says, pushing her glass towards me, "You see my glass is on empty. Ya better put that tiger back in my tank!" So I laugh a little. And I pick up the nearly empty bottle and pour Mama the last of the truth cocktail. "Thank Ya!" Mama says, with a nod and a flash of a smile.

"Mr. Hunt was a good boss. Sometimes he's kinda stern, but always fair. And do you know that man taught me, a woman with only a ninth grade education how to do HIS books Annie Mae…Me?" Mama says, patting her finger against her chest. And he owns three other bars on the South Side; I wind up doing those books too." Mama sits her glass down and stares at me, with red rim eyes.

"Whatever a boss or a teacher has ta show you, you take that Annie Mae, and ya learn from it. Don't walk around pretending like ya already know it," Mama says, justa crunching and smacking on her ice. "Take that learning and put it in yo breast pocket, you'll need it someday."

I slide down into my seat until my knees are nearly touching Mama's. And I watch Mama sip on that truth cocktail. And that burning confidence is nudging at my belly again, nudging at my tongue again. And I tuck in my lips trying my best to keep them shut, before I know it, I ask, "While you're doing all of this bar keeping and bookkeeping, where's Daddy," I say, watching Mama with zoom lenses.

"Oh Child please," Mama says waving her hand, and crunching down on more ice. "That man finds out where I'm working after a few months, and he comes looking for me. He shows me his arms, and their all smooth, almost shiny, golden brown, and the old needle marks are all but faded away. And he shows me his pay stub, telling me he's working for the rail road now. "I wants you back, Selma," he says, and his eyes sorta glisten with guilt. "I know I did you and Gloria wrong. But I'm a different man now Baby and I want us ta be a family again."

"And then he looks around at the bar and at the type of people in there, and he looks back at me, smacking his teeth and says, "Sides, you ain't got no bizness working in no bar." What did that motha-fucka say that for? He was doing fine and had me feeling just about dandy till he says that."

"And I cock my head at that man, and I lay my bitchiness on the table, and I say, "I HAD ta make it MY bizness. Hell, you sho didn't make it yours, now did ya? Yo only bizness was stabbing a damn needle up yo vein. Now ya wanna come up in heah, and whisk me away like I'm so kinda got-damn Cinderella." I scan him up and down with a quick flash and I say, "Take yo sorry ass and yo sorry pay check up outta my face." And I point towards the open door and shake my head and say, "Now, blaze the trail motha-fucka!"

"Why did you do that Mama," I ask, with question marks in my eyes.

"Hmmp," Mama says, sloshing her ice and the last bit of liquor around in the glass. "Three times that man came for me. And three times I sent his ass away.

"Hmmp, I'm like a burnt child Annie Mae, I dread the very thought of a fire. So I put our marriage and our love on the back burner. Besides, I can't be no easy fish for no motha-fucka, Annie Mae." Mama says shaking her hand and pointing at her chest, "Ugh-ugh, not Miss Selma." And again, I notice a yellow mask of light making itself at home on Mama's face.

Then Mama takes in a long, last swig of that truth cocktail, and says, "Everythang is going a long pretty good in that bar for about a year or so, and then one night, I'll never forget, the sun is falling down from the sky. And Baby in all my years down south I ain't never seen a prettier sun-set than the one I see in Chicago that night. The sun looks like a burning flame. It's all orange and pink like. And I look across at the open door, and the buildings outside have long sheets of that pinkish orange flame stretching across the red and brown bricks. And the doorway…the doorway Annie Mae, has a long welcome mat of that same orange and pink flame shining right down in front of it." Mama says, then she strains her eyes and takes the tips of her fingers and squeezes her lips tightly together (and I can't help but to wonder if Mama is trying to squeeze that truth out or squeeze it back in).

And Mama's fingers ease away from her lips and she says, "I help Mr. Hunt make a few changes around there. Now at all of the side tables there are checkered table cloths and little red glasses holding candles. So I am sitting at one of the side tables working on the books by candle light, and I'm looking up justa admiring this pretty sunset. And I put my head back down penciling in a number. And I lift my head back up. And ain't nothing there Annie Mae, nothing but dark sky. Then the street lights come on. And lo and behold I see this big, long limo cruising up to the curb. All black and shiny like, with the street lights gleaming off the chrome. And baby it was the oddest thang, not one chauffer gets outta that car, but two, one on both sides, two big, black, cock-strong looking motha-fuckas, with their hat bibs justa shining on their heads. And they rush toward the trunk of the car. One opens the trunk, and the other one starts pulling something heavy and chrome-like out. And the other one helps him. And it's a wheelchair Annie Mae, a big, monster looking thang. Look like it can hold two or, three people.

And they walk at a brisk pace and one opens up the side door of the limo. And I see this one watermelon, dress wearing thigh poke out through the darkness, and then the other thigh swings out. And the two chauffeurs go to work again. They take off the side panels of the chair. And with a huh and a hmmp they help this big, 400 lb looking woman into this wheel chair. And the woman is so big the sides of her hips just swing, and flap, off the sides the wheel chair. And she's a mulatto looking woman, with a big print dress on and this iddy biddy hat with cherries on it. And the hat looks so funny on top of this big woman's head, with these three or fo chins above her neck. And her dark brown hair hangs across her shoulders and curls up a little bit at the ends. And I just KNOW they ain't even gonna try and bring two-ton Tammie up in heah! "

And baby, sho-nuff, they wheel her to the bottom of the stairs. And one of the chauffeurs gets in front. And they both dig in their pockets and pull out these heavy looking leather gloves, and they both put them on, flexing their hands and fingers. And Baby befo' I know it the one in front is stooping down and grabbing hold of those front wheels. "Ya got it," he says to the one in back.

"Yeah I got it." And BOOM…BOOM…BOOM, they're lifting that heavy woman up those steps. "Hold it…Hold it, hands slipping," the one in front grunts.

"Ya got it," the one in back asks.

"Yeah!" he answers. BOOM…BOOM…BOOM!

"And after each step the cherries on that woman's head wobbles, her head shakes, and the flab on her arms jiggles. But baby it's something about this heah woman, the way she sits up high in that wheelchair. Pride has wrapped it's self around her like a python! Baby that woman is a high baller and a shot caller! And her eyes Annie Mae, her eyes are on me, like cold on ice. When they bump her over the last curve, the wheel chair is so wide, it can barely fit in the doorway. And the man in the back is trying his best ta make it fit. And I look at the wheels and I can see the paint chips justa flying off the corners of the doorway. Once he gets her in, he wheels her towards me. And with a flick of her hand, and gravel in her voice, she says "I'll take it from here boys". And they stand at the doorway with there feet spread apart, and their hand behind there back, like licorice dipped solders. She takes her fingers and wheels herself up to me and befo I know it, I'm on my feet and standing in the middle of the bar. And her eyes never leave my eyes. And she gets near me and she stops dead on a pebble. A cunning smile creeps across her face and she backs that wheel chair up with those flabby arms….and BAM she races the foot pedal strait into my left ankle. And that pain shoots through me like a rifle. And before I know it I draw back my fist, and it's ready to swing like a windmill. That heifer knows exactly what she's doing! And something says "Hold it.... Wait just a damn minute. You didn't dress that woman before she left home. She can have a gun, knife, or anythang underneath that dress with YO name on it…Slow down…Take it easy. So I hold on to my temper and my fist."

And baby, that woman throws back her head and places her hand on her big belly and laughs. And that laugh fills her belly, travels to her throat, tears her eyes, floats across the room, and back down into her belly again. "WHOOAH" she says, wiping the tears from her eyes. "So you're the flavor of the moment? Heyyy Lee, this one is kinda on the dark side ain't she? I thought you said chocolate breaks you out?" That woman says, and they're talking about me as if I ain't even there. "What did he tell ya sweetie", the woman asked. "Did he tell you this was all his?" "If it wasn't for me he couldn't even wipe his own ass", that bitch says, with her eyes and lips crinkling up to laugh again.

And Annie Mae, I look over at Mr. Hunt. And he's over on the other side of the bar, pretending like he's shelving in-ven-tory. But believe me when I tell you, that man's over there shelving a lot mo than just inventory. Not looking at me, not defending me, not doing NOTHING for me, but sucking on that tooth-pick.

And I wanna straddle that wheel chair, and straddle that big bitch. I wanna strangle her fat ass till she can't laugh or shake no mo. I wanna strangle herrr till her eyes pop out of her head, and her bluish tongue lags to the side."

And I look over at Mama's eyes and their empty. I look down at Mama's hands and they're clutching the now empty glass. And she's justa shaking it…and she won't stop shaking it. And my eyes dart back to her eyes… they're still empty. And Mama's justa mumbling, mumbling words I can't understand, mumbling words I'm not sure I want to understand." What happened then Mama" I shout, popping my hand on the table.

Mama jumps, "Ooh Child", she says heaving a big sigh of the past, and finally setting her empty glass on the table. "I look at her and then over at Mr. Hunt one last time, and I half run and half limp outta that bar. And I keep on running with that stinging ankle. And I can still hear that fat woman laughing at me. I run and I run till I can't hear her laughing no more. And about a block or two away I catch the side of this building with one hand and my ankle with the other. And I just let my head crumble into the side of that building. And my ankle hurts so bad. My lungs hurts so bad… but most of all, most of all, my pride hurts so bad", Mama whispers, biting down hard on her lip and her pass.

My eyes travel up from the table and I look up at Mama's eyes. Her eyes look into my eyes. And it's as if a coffin of dirt has been lifted from my eyes. And I'm seeing daylight… sunlight for the first time. And now I can't see nothing but Mama, I can't hear nothing but Mama. I slide into a puddle of Mamas. I'm swimming in a sea of Mamas I'm drowning in a sea of Mamas "Mama", I say, coming up for air, and coming up for the truth! "Is Mr. Hunt my real daddy?" I ask with a croak.

Mama rests her face in one hand and drums the other one on the table, and says with a bored sigh, "I'm putting it where a fool can understand it". And Lord, Lord, Lord, what did she say that for? Before I know it, my anger leaps to the floor, my feet leap to the floor, and I leap frog over to Mama with hurling hands and hurling accusations. And I'm all up in Mama's face. "You LIED to me! You ain't nothing but a frigging LIAR!" And I pretended not to notice the fire works that spark in Mama's eyes.

Now I don't know about your family, but in mines, you'd stand a better chance of doing a water dance with a plugged in toaster than calling your mother a liar. But I don't stop, that burning confidence was drooling at my lips, babbling at my mouth, it won't let me stop… it's feeling too good to stop! "All my life ain't been NOTHING but one big LIE! A LIE you shoved in my face… You breast fed me that lie… then you spoon fed me that….!" BASH…! Brown shards of glass and anger fly this way and that way to the floor. Mama rises from her chair like a monster from the sea, with that now jagged liquor bottle justa swinging and those red eyes justa bulging.

And Lord I wanna run. I know I should run. But I can't run, that burning confidence has packed its bag and left town, and fear has my feet stapled to the floor! Mama jerks me by my hair and slings me close to her face, so close I can see her pores, and she puts that bottle near my throat (Near My Throat Jesus) and says in a low voice, so low I can barely hear her. "As long as yo blood bleeds red, don't you EVER call me a liar! Do you hear me?" She says, with her alcohol breath playing on my face, I shitted yo ass out Bitch. And I won't think two SHITS, about erasing yo ass from the fucking game!"

Then Mama tightens her grip on my hair and jerks my head as hard as she can, so hard a pain slaps from one side of my neck to the other. And Mama's liquor filled eyes look at me with hate, a foaming at the mouth kinda hate. A hate that makes her want to kill me dead. "I ain't never wanted yo black ass Bitch. You hear me, NEVER! I wanted yo ass dead bitch. I wanted your ass as dead as a got-damn skeleton! I tried pills", she says shaking the liquor bottle in my face and shaking my head, "Pills that were supposed to bring down my period! Pills that didn't do nothing! NOTHING"! She screams shaking my head and spitting in my face.

Mama looks up and her eyes glaze with something from the past, something I can't see, something I can't reach. "He told me," she says almost mumbling, "he told me he didn't want no babies. I believed him Jesus, I believed him Lord! I was sooo young… I didn't know, I didn't know, that the mutha-fucka was putting pin holes in the rubber…holes that filled me up with YOU…You"! Mama's eyes get as big as silver dollars, and every time she says 'you' she bangs my head on the table. WHOP…WHOP…WHOP! Mama's hate filled eyes search my eyes for pain, search my eyes to see if my water pipes are leaking. I ain't gonna give her what she wants. I'll take the pain…I'll take the blame. But she won't take pleasure in my tears.

Mama slams to her knees then and slams me down with her…I lay still as a picture-in-a-frame, not saying nothing… Not doing nothing! "You wanted the truth bitch… Now suck on it! Suck on the got-damn hard candy of truth BITCH! Suck on it! Ahhhh, but it goes down kinda hard don't it" Mama says, banging my head to the floor. And a bolt of pain flashes before my eyes. Eyes that can't show her I'm in pain… Eyes that WON'T show her I'm in pain.

"You brought shame upon me Bitch…shame upon my husband that didn't want you…and no longer wanted me…but tried his damnest to accept my mistake. My MISTAKE," Mama wails! "Who wants an ugly-ass tar baby bitch…? Whoooo", Mama asks, spitting in my face, waving the jagged edges of that liquor bottle in my face. "Answer me Bitch…I said answer MEEE!"

The only answer Mama gets is the commercial on the radio… *"How do ya handle a hungry mannnnn… the man handlers, man handlers!"*

Mama's hair flops over her face like a sheep dog, she takes in hard and heavy breathes, breathes from the past, breathes that can't erase the past

Her twisted face hovers over mine, like a witch in a fairy tale. And with mashed in lips and slits for eyes, she lifts the liquor bottle high above her head and she slings shots through the air. It slices through the room, over the T.V set and lands on the carpet near the brass floor lamp. And that brown bottle spins and scrapes, scrapes and spins against the brass... SPSS... SPSS…SPSS….SPSS. And I shut my eyes and heave a sigh of relief.

And she lets go of me now. But she doesn't let go of the past. She watches the spinning of that bottle. And that bottle takes Mama back…back to the far side of nowhere. I quietly scoot from underneath Mama and I find the safety of a nearby corner. And Mama raises her hands up and balls her fists up and says, "All I ever needed was my beautiful, beautiful light skinned Gloria with her silky long hair. That's all I ever needed…Jesus, and You gave that to meee! That's all I ever needed…"and Mama grabs hold to herself and she rocks herself…back and forward…forward and back. "All I ever wanted…all I ever needed…was my beautiful…beautiful Gloria….." And Mama rocks and rocks…and her voice gets lower and lower, until it's nothing more than a silent prayer.

I tuck my knees up to my chest, and I lay my head on my knees, and I cry now, tears that are the size of bullets! I cry for my Mama now, the Mama I ain't never really had…But I know, as sure as I know that MY skin is black, that one day, one day it'll be Mama's turn to cry for ME…Annie Mae, the black, ugly child, she ain't never really wanted.

OOOH and I KNOW…I just KNOW that my Mama doesn't really hate ME…she don't hate me, she hates herself! When she sees my big lips…she sees herself…when she sees my kinky hair …she sees herself…when she sees my black skin…she sees herself. HERSELF (and I pound on my leg)…HERSELF (I pound on my thigh) …HERSELF...! HERSELF...! HERSELF!

Part VII

1976

Mama packs her madness into a suitcase and heads back to Chicago. I bury mine in a garden called hope, and I head towards tomorrow. I move into the Webster Hotel, which is between 34th street and 9th avenue. They call this area Hell's kitchen, but nowadays the only thing hellish about is the traffic. 9th Avenue is littered with old buildings with rusty fire escapes and fruit stands run by old men with scraggly beards.

And yes, I'm accepted at Julliard. And yes, regardless of the pot liquor of pain Mama has forced me to gulp down, I still gotta click in my heels and a glide in my stride. Because you see, I feel like a seed. I've been buried down so low, I ain't got no place to go but up!

Now before I go any further, I think I should tell you that back in those days, Julliard didn't have housing for its students. So like I said, I move into the Webster Hotel an all women housing facility. There must be nearly 800 women up in here.

And I feel as if they're all pieces of Annie Mae. Women who have come here to taste their fortune, to grab hold of their fame. And ohh I tell you, I feel like I'm rocking in the bosom of artistry. They have artists here, sculptresses there, dancers to the right of me, jazz singers to the left of me, writers to the north of me, and musicians to the south of me.

Being in my little room I don't get to see them much. Ooh but child, be it dinner time or breakfast time the divas are on the prowl. Dancers who walk with their bodies erect, with their hair pinned back with pins and poise. Musicians who can't walk unless there's a music case thumping at their sides, painters with splashes of art on their jeans, hands and hair. Writers who sit at the table with endless cups of coffee and cigarettes welded to their fingers.

All my life I've been told what to do, and how to do it. And Julliard ain't no better. It's nothing but a Nuevo Selma with a Nuevo attitude. They tell me what to drink to improve my voice. They tell me what to eat to improve my voice. They tell me what exercises to do to improve my voice. They tell me to learn German. They tell me to learn Italian- - I'm in a cesspool of discipline, and Lord knows I want to get out. But still, I'm in the Big Apple now child and I'm ready to chomp that bad boy down to the core!

Walking down the long dark hallways of school is like walking into a wall of noise. In one room horns are seeping out the doors. From another corner a baritone voice bellows from the mortar. Further down the clang of a Steinway flows through the walls. Even further down you can hear another piano banging out chords, with a teacher ordering, "Ple-as and rel-le-ves ", to the beat of the piano.

Now God knows if I never see another dance teacher for as long as I'm black, it would be fine by me. But Julliard feels that opera singers also need grace and movement. So I'm stuck with this damn dance teacher, Madame so-called Zarnovska. And they give out more lies about that woman than Disco gives out hits. They say that Madame is from Russia, and that she danced with the Bolshoi Ballet. They say she's first cousin to Rudolph Nureyev. They say…they say…they say! Child they had strung that string of lies about that woman so tight you can just about choke on it. Hmmp, she wasn't fooling me, in my mind her real name is Sally Polowski, from East Orange New Jersey. And the closest she has come to the Bolshoi Ballet was at Delores' school of tap on the corner of 5 3 rd and nowhere. She may have the other students fooled, but I can see right through Madame, like saran wrap.

Madame steps into the classroom with this "it's all about me dahling" attitude. Her face is a road map of wrinkles…a road map of time. Her hair is pulled back into a black turban, with a white blond mane that curls into a page boy at her shoulders, white blonde hair that snatches up glints of light from the ceiling. Madame carries a black cane with a pearl handle. A cane that captures the piano beat, a cane that will whack you into discipline, a cane that will stomp you into discipline.

All the students are at the bar, in front of the mirror doing stretches, with one agonizing leg on the bar and the other one tree stomped to the wooden floor. We're looking in the mirror that circles the floor. And I guess we're all wondering how we can make it hurt some more, because if it don't hurt hey, it just it don't work. So it's gotta hurt… and it's gotta hurt good. Women with Danskin bodies stretch into a strange "C" curve, with their dark hair spilling across the bar. Men with buzz cuts and tailor made muscles squat and lift at the bar.

Madame stretches out her sleeves, sleeves that drape like bat wings and taps the cane on the wooden floor…tap…tap…tap…tap. "Let us begin…assume thee position". She says in her phony Russian accent. She claps her hands, and nods at the timid little piano player, that sits in a narrow corner of the room. He looks like a panic attack that's waiting to happen. He's a small dainty, little something. It looks as if that large black piano can swallow that man whole.

Well, we all take our stretched out, pulled out legs off the bar. And our sweat heaving bodies stand straight against the bar with our feet pointing north and south. We look like a flock of waddling and quacking ducks.

And sure enough Madame's watery blue eyes zoom in on me like radar. And that damn cane points straight at me like Geiger counter. And her leather point shoes follow. "Ah-na", she says (just refusing to call me by my real name), "You are out of alignment", she says with that damn cane pushing and poking up my back. "Let your back remain straight, like it's sweeping up towards the stars". And that damn woman shoots that cane up my back, like a cannon ball! She better collect some sense and leave me the hell alone! And I turn my head towards that woman, and I shoot daggers from my eyes. Her snake like body slinks towards the next student (victim). Acting like she doesn't see me, but that heifer sees me alright!

I ain't gonna sit here and tell you that she doesn't treat the other students the same way she does me, because she does. But it's just something about that cane jabbing and nabbing at me all the time. It makes me wanna go cannibal on her behind!

That evening on the Broadway bus headed home, I hear two students that are members of the congregation of the church of Madame Zarnovska. Looking more like they just stepped foot off of a Idaho potato farm, than they do dancers. They're in the halleluiah corner, justa testifying, and sanctifying the praises of Madame Zarnovska. The only thing missing is a tambourine and a collection plate. "Did you hear that at one time her and Margot Fonteyne were roommates?" asked one of them, standing in a tight space in the back of the bus.

"Why yes I did!" begins the other. "Can you imagine the secrets they must have shared? Oh, I would give anything to have been a fly on That wall. And I've also been told that her and Martha Graham have been the best of friends for the last twenty years". She says cutting her eyes at me, and I roll my eyes back at her.

Child please, the closest that woman has come to Martha is munching on a cracker… a damn graham cracker. "Oh she's such a marvel," the other student begins. "I get more from her one class than I do from three or four. I don't know how I'm gonna fit her into my class schedule next semester, but I'm going to do it, if I have to walk on broken glass". He says holding on to the bus pole swaying back and forward. His friend bobs her pony tailed head, and squints her eyes in agreeable laughter. Madame is good alright. She has them all fooled, but she isn't fooling me. She's as fake as a floating guru.

The next day in class Madame has us doing floor exercises. Our legs spread with our hands and chins touching the floor (almost in a "W" shape). The pianist beats out the chords. And Madame follows suit with the cane pounding on the floor. "One…two… three…four…let your arms stretch! Stretch….stretch… stretch! She orders… Boom…Boom…Boom!

And Lord have mercy, sure enough Madame zooms in on me…again. Stop the music", she orders swooping up one draping arm. And that God forsaken cane points to me (her Geiger counter) again. And it leads her to me.

"Ah-na" she begins. And all I see are her leather point shoes, pointing to the side of my mouth. "You must open your legs wider; open them up as though you're receiving a man". And Madame has the emancipated gall to take that cane and sweep my legs wide open. And a crocodile of pain bites into my thighs!

But Madame isn't satisfied with just doing that, she's at a buffet table called authority. And I'm the appetizer. Miss Thing from New Jersey takes that damn cane and pushes it, and presses it into the small of MY frigging back talking about, "you must press farther … farther down." Well hell I can't press down any further! My lips are already kissing the damn floor. What did she do that for? "As if you're connected----". Oh I'm ready to connect alright! Connect my foot right up yo…..!

And Bam! Before I know it my hands are swinging around that cane! That cane Miss Thing refuses to let go of. That cane I REFUSE to let go of…That cane that seems to lift me up on my feet...That cane that has me swinging and twisting toe to toe with this woman…eye to eye, with this woman. That cane that her white and blue lined claws won't let go of. That cane that I refuse to let go of. Her red rimmed eyes look at me with surprise. My eyes look at her with determination. Why won't that heifer just let go…let go heifer! And let me break this damn cane. And that will be the end of it. You better let go, before I break it over your damn head! I say to myself. But this old bird is strong, as strong as 5 gallons of Jack damn Daniels.

Oh it's on now…it's on… alright Miss Sally…Miss Sally Polanski from New Jersey, Because that's your real name, you ain't foolin me, I say to myself. You're gonna have to give it up. And turn it loose. And I push my weight against that sister. I am determine to get that damn cane. And the cane goes up to her saggin, tissue paper neck. And I'll shake this cane from this sister. Or I'll shake her brains outta her head. And I bite down on my lips and my strength and place all my weight on sister's feet. And I shake that cane and that heifer one…good…time…!

And Lord, Lord what did I do that for! That turban and that blond hair lifts from that woman's head and flies across the room like a flying sauce, justa twisting and turning. And the pageboy that's sewn to the turban is floating out like wings. And all eyes are sealed to this turban as it flies across the piano and spins, hovers across the pianist's head like a ceiling fan. And his chrome dome and eyes are justa spinning and twirling looking at it.

And it lands nicely on top of that man's head… "AHHHHHHH",and he lets out a girlish scream. And with a wagging tongue, and wagging hands he zooms up outta his flying chair. He's twisting and shouting, like he's being whacked with a cattle prod! And he's doing the dance of the three stooges, trying to get that monstrosity off his head.

And we all look at the wig that sits on the floor like a dead spider. And a painful Ooooh…lifts from the students mouths. And for one minute…one long minute, time becomes an old lady. An old lady with a walker, an old lady that can barely move, barely walk, barely make it, step….. walker…..step….walker….stepping along. And all of the students' eyes are bulging. And all the students' mouths are gaping at that wig…plastered to that wig, plastered in time.

And with a dead man's weight all eyes turn towards Madame. And what I see …Lord I rather be blind…than to see what I see. Madame is standing there grabbing her nearly bald head. Grey threads of hair sprout from that woman's fingers, like the roots from a turnip.

And the truth hits me then. The truth hits me like an extension cord…Whop! And I know as sure as I know that I came from my mother's womb that this woman is dying. That death has been pecking at her window for a long, long time. I don't know how I know, but I just know and that turban, that wig, that cane, that pride, that arrogance…was just her way. Her way of keeping a seal on that tightly closed window! But I had put a hole in that seal. I chose to snatch that away from this woman. She didn't mean no harm…she never meant anyone no harm! Her watery blue eyes look into my eyes and ask, a thousand and one times, "why?". And my eyes say to her eyes," I didn't know …I'm sorry…so sorry".

But you see being sorry isn't going to give this woman her dignity back. Sorry isn't going to add years to her life. And sorry sure ain't gonna put hair back on this woman's head. Because sorry ain't never did nothing for nobody, but put flowers on their grave!
Madame's eyes brim with anger. And she slams her cane to the floor. And the clang of the cane rings across the floor boards, drifts upwards and downwards from the walls, and the ceiling and slips, into the attic of my guilty conscience.

And with one grand sweep Madame shakes her head and snaps a blue print scarf from around her neck. And with eyes that are candle waxed into mine, she wraps and twists and twist and wraps that scarf around her head…she wraps and pulls, until it looks more like hair than a scarf. Hair that balls in the back, hair that braids from the sides to the front… hair of blue, gold and pink.

And with trembling lips and narrow eyes she looks down at the cane, up at me, and down at the cane again. And with one tip of her pointed shoe, she rolls the cane over to me. And the black lacquer shines and gleams, rolling, and a twisting towards me. And it stops … stops at my feet, like a trained dog. But I don't want it anymore. I swear to God… I don't want it! And I back away from it, like it's the Ebola virus.

Madame reaches for her fringed black cape that's on a nearby folding chair and she swoops it around her shoulders. And the fringes on the bottom shake with a new found dignity. And she sails to the door with her cape floating behind her. And I just KNOW that the door is gonna slam. But Madame closes that door with an almost silent click.

I'm so ashamed, a shame that lashes and welts at the bottom of my legs, pulls and jerks at my thighs, twists and turns and curves and stings up towards my waists, and it bites, gnaws, and burns at my face. And I try to take in a long, deep breath of that shame as I turn around and face the other students. But they're not students anymore. They become a sea of hands. Hands that cup to ears…whispering, hands that cup to mouths…snickering, hands that cup to jaws… judging.

I snatch up my bag, my coat, and my courage. And I run from that room. I run from that school. I run from that truth. And I try to run from myself… and I do too…I hide at the bottom of a liquor bottle.

Part VIII

I ain't got nothing Jesus! Do you hear me…Nothing! But the fear that grows like hairs on the back of my head. And the pain that I use as a chaser in my liquor! You've left me with pure-dee NOTHING! I ain't got school, after what I did Julliard doesn't want me anymore. I ain't got a mother that loves me. I ain't never had a Daddy. I ain't got nothing…Do you hear me? I ain't got nothing!

I'm sitting here in my little room, on my little bed at the Webster House. It's been three days since Julliard sent me that prim and proper letter, telling me oh-so politely, that they don't want me anymore! Now, I just KNEW even before I opened the damn letter that they didn't want anymore.

And I sit here, and I read this letter, over and over again. Because what I didn't know is …seeing the words printed up so nicely on this beige parchment paper, I didn't know that the words are like spikes Jesus, spikes that cut and tear at my fingers! Spikes that won't let me breathe, spikes that gag at my throat and I can't do a thing about it, but let my tears plop and drop to this paper. And I watch those printed words melt like hot cheese. Oh but you see, the pain can't melt. And I ask myself what went wrong over and over again. But the only answer I get is another sip of alcohol slipping down my throat.

I look out the window at the grey, wet afternoon. And I listen to the rain dropping and popping on the sides of the building, whooshing, and sloshing from the trucks and cars on the street below. And I can't help but to think back a couple of weeks ago, when I looked out this very same window. Only I don't see rain falling from the sky on this particular day. I see human pain falling…human pain like I ain't ever seen it before. And I pray to God that I never see it again…I see a blonde haired woman free falling from the twelfth floor of this very building. And I want to jump back from the window. But I can't, I'm nailed to the scene, like a martyr to the Cross. And all I can do is stand here and bear witness to her persecution. I watch that poor child jump to her very death, jump to her so-called freedom.

And Lord, Lord, I remember her eyes Jesus. For one scrap of a second, I remember her eyes speaking to me. There is calmness there in her blue eyes. A don't cry for me kinda calmness, a calmness I never seen nor heard before, a calmness that tears at my heart and drops it to the floor. There is no fear of the pavement in those blue eyes, just calmness. And then her body tumbles, her hair swirls and her bell bottom pants flap. And she's gone. I can't see her anymore…I don't want to see her anymore. She's gone without a cry, gone without a whimper, gone without a scream…she's gone…just gone!

And I often wonder what brought that poor child to that breaking point. They tell me her life was as bright and pretty as a diamond (isn't that what they say about most people in that situation?). She was a rising artist who had just had a show down in Soho. But if her life was so bright and pretty how come she's dead now? And how come after you're dead and can't defend yourself, people try to drape and pin flowers on your life. They like to sprinkle pretty words as if they were rose petals, across your headstone? Words, they would have NEVER have said if you were alive. Words you NEED to hear when you're alive, healing words, soothing words, Red Cross words!

People kill me, when they get up and call themselves eulogizing about the dead, but hell, they didn't live YOUR life, and they sure as hell can't paint-by-numbers your life! And they call that respect…respect for the dead. And it seems to me that maybe…just maybe, that child could have had a better life if they showed some respect while she was living.

And I ain't going no place in New York, no place but crazy. "Cause I can't help but to feel, like I did FEEL something of that poor child's life. I feel like there's something, something living in the corners of this old, brick building, something that got a hold to that child. Now I feel like it's trying it's best to get a hold of me too. Something that licks at pain and loneliness…..Fear!

It bangs at the walls at night, but only the broken and the weak can hear it. But I hear her and I know her. Her name is FEAR (and I know all this is crazy, but its how I feel). Fear of wondering how I'm going to free flow through another day, without breaking apart. The kind of fear that spreads across my morning toast, snuggles in my bed at night, a fear that pits and pats at my heels when I cross a busy street, a fear of never learning who I really am. A fear of not EVER being loved or giving love…fear of going home a failure… FEAR…FEAR…FEAR!

Oooh I just know that if I don't hurry up and get outta this building get outta this city, that they'll be eulogizing me pretty soon. Because you see, they call this "The Big Apple". But what they don't tell you is that there's a big, worm living inside of this apple. And if you ain't strong, hard, or careful it's just waiting, waiting to suck you dry.

And New York ain't a city at all, if it ain't a city of the lost. So many young girls just like me have come to this city to stand in audition lines, only to wind up standing in the welfare line with a fist full of lost dreams and lost hope. And the only way they can find a piece of that dream is through a one night stand, a high paying trick, or sometimes a wrist full of needle marks, or if they really want a way out they swallow a fist full of pills.

I KNOW now that I ain't bad enough to take on this giant worm. And it senses my fear and I KNOW…I just KNOW that it's waiting for me and salivating for me, with a wagging tongue and gaping jaws! Oh, I've got to go home; I've got to go home …or I'm body bag bound!

Part IX

Circa 1979

Now you probably stay on the North side, the decent side, the safe side, but me, I stay on the South side, the gritty side, the desperate side, and sometimes the hateful side…but still it's my side. I live above a lounge, at the corner of 79th and Cottage Grove. A lounge called the Blue Dahlia. And I tend bar at this lounge too. And Honey, some of the sweetest blues pours outta this joint, like hot syrup on pancakes! And a whole lotta white folks and Uptown college kids venture over here to hear this one particular bluesman do-his-do, and mix up his tantalizing brew, because he's one thing that the North Side doesn't have. I'm talking about Shady Grady and his Blues Mercedes!

Ohh I tell you, I tell YOU, Shady Grady loves to wear his cowboy get-up on stage. And the audience will lean in as close as they can to that stage, trying their best to get a piece of his blues voodoo, because his blues gris-gris, and his blues mojo be shonuf' working! The blue lightning will come down and flash on that man like a thunderbolt! And he'll lean that body back and that cowboy head back, and with tightly shut eyes, he'll strike a chord on that guitar, just one chord now, and it'll sizzle through you like hot grease! And he'll open up one eye, just one eye and cut it around, just to make sure he's got ya where he wants ya. And that Jeri-curled head of his will start to swinging, and his bottom lip will start to quiver. And that guitar….Lord, that Guitar will shonuf' get that body to quaking and shaking. And his fingers will slide up and down the neck of that guitar, like he's making love to a skinny- legged woman. And his other hand will stroke a one note cord on the strings. And he'll lift that hand up, like Moses holding up the Blues

Commandments. And all the while the electric blue lights are curving and swerving across that man's body, like a demon aura!

And you'll hear some man in the corner shout, "Play it Grady, goddammit, I say play it!"

And some little shriveled up lady with her shriveled up dreams will raise her dress and let her legs shake and rattle like ice water. And the audience will stand back and give this lil' shriveled up sister some room. And sure enough a whiskeyed up fella will start feeling Grady's shonuf' groove and joins in with her. And he'll throw back his head, showing a crown of bad teeth, and he'll laugh a don't-care laugh, and he'll pull shriveled-up sister real close and they move on and they groove on.

And the Blues Mercedes is riding the beat train hard and wild. The drummer man finds religion on those cymbals. And he shuts his eyes and pouts his mouth and catches the sanctified, funktified, shonuf' banging beat. The bass man puts his back into it, and with his legs and feet going one way and his guitar going the other way, he looks like a "Z" reject from Sesame Street.

And from out of the darkness steps a short-haired, light-skinned sister. And she's a tiny wisps of a thing, looks like if you breathe to heavy you can blow her down. She snatches up that microphone so hard the pedestal is just a whirling and a twirling. And she frowns up her face and gives the audience a "You make me SICK," scowl, and she tilts back her head and growls, like a shonuf' man, "*WELLLLL, ya left meee pretty Baby, but aye don't care at all! I said ya left meeee pretty Baby, but aye don't care at ALL!*" And her hips and lips shake like food in a processor. And her free hand just misses her crotch and she groans, "*'Cause since you left me pretty Baby, me and my thighs....have been having a BALL!*"

And the men in the audience hoop and holler. But lil' Sister ain't finished yet. She bends at the knees and her body gets almost as low as her voice and she testifies, "*WELLLL, you weren't nothing Baby, but a Minute-man. Welll, yoouuuu weren't nothing Baby, but a Minute-man. And now I take it nice and slow and get alllll the lovin I can!*" And this time, all the women in the audience whoop and holler! And her body snakes and wiggles as she stands back up.

And Grady and his guitar slides in right along side of her. His fingers slide and glide across that guitar while his eyes slide and glide across lil' sister. Her body hoochies and coochies, answering to the call of the blues, and her lips pucker and she swings one hand to the back of her neck, and she waves the micro phoned hand in the air.

And her body shakes on down and her head tosses that beat around. And every time the guitar slides and glides, sister answers with her own hutti-gutti, smutti-gutti slide and glide.

"Ahhhh Christine, Christine, don't ya be so mean," begs one man.

"Ahhh, work it and jerk it Baby, just work it and jerk it," demands another.

And what did he say that for? Ms. Christine works her mouth into a sour pickle pout, jumps from the stage and grabs that very man by his waist and slides and grinds on his leg like it's a fire house pole. And the audience backs up and makes room with an "OOOOhhhhh…." on their lips. And that poor man can't do nothing but raise up his hands and enjoy the ride. And then Christine takes her hands and slides them up and down on that man's chest like she's giving him a sex vapor rub. And she arches her back as far as she can, until her head almost sweeps across the floor. And the only thing that's touching that man is her groin and thighs. And Lord knows that poor man just can't takes no mo! He bites down on his lower lip, shuts his eyes, clutches her waist and starts grinding sister right back. And Christine stops dead cold, and looks up at that man like he's a rat turd. And she pivots on her heels and ego, and gives off that special, "You want this," wiggle and jiggle. She climbs back onto the stage and continues to wail with the band. And that poor man has that, "What the hell just happened," frown on his face. And the audience pours back into the middle. And a few men give his shoulders a pity pat. And that's how it is every night at the Blue Dahlia Lounge.

But this one particular night, about a year later is so different. And although the A.C. is running full blast there's an unbearable heat in the bar, a kinda yanking at yo clothes kinda heat. And there's a peculiar stench that rest right below that heat, a sour, almost vinegar like smell. Everyone is so different and so angry and Christine is so different too. She's late coming on stage, which is something she will never do. And she acts like the audience isn't even there. She walks up to the edge of the stage and careens her neck, squints her eyes, and she sees somebody out there, a special somebody. And she sucks in a deep breath and it seems as if she refuses to let it go. And she takes a couple of steps back (almost stumbling back), she slowly shakes her head and bites down on her lip as if she's biting down on a hard piece of regret. And a cloud of pain covers that child's face, a cloud I ain't never seen on her before. Confident Christine is gone. And in its place is a confused, almost child-like little something. She shakes her head again and she turns and whispers something to Shady Grady.

And Grady nods his head and takes hold of the mike and says, "We gone do it a little differently for y'all tonight. We're going down; all the way down home y'all. We gonna give y'all a taste of the real blues, the low-down Mississippi, pot lickin' Delta Blues. And we're gonna put the blue back into the blues." And every song that child sings, it isn't bumping and thumping, there all slow and low. She sings about the good times she let get away, and how she allowed all the bad times to stay. Christine sings about stirring the blues into her morning coffee, and how it lumps up on her pillow at night. And after each song she sorta shakes her head, and her eyes glaze over with regret. And you can just TELL that she's singing all of this to one somebody in the audience.

And I notice that there's a new customer in the bar that night, someone I had never seen before. He's a lone dark-skinned man, with slick back hair, and he sits at the bar with a freshly pressed white suit on. He sits there sipping on his whiskey, puffing deep and hard on his cigs, with a knowing squint in his eyes. And Christine moves her hips with a slow desperate groove. And it seems to me like the smoke from that man's cigarette is dancing, swaying, and flaying right along with that girl.

And at one point that child is begging so hard for that man's love, she snatches the mike from the stand, falls to her knees, and bends at the waist like she's about to hurl up all of love's pain, all of love's injustice! And that girl hollers, *"Further on down that road you're gonna finnnd you're the one for me. Further on down that road, you're gonna find you're the one for MEEEEE. WELL, WELL, remember that I told ya that I love ya, a love that WILL ALLLLWAYS BEEEEE. WHOAH, you're gonna find that you're the one for me. Just can't forget ya pretty Baby, and I'mmmm so tired of trying. OOOOHHHH, I just can't forget ya pretty Baby, and I'm so TIRED of TRYING. NAW…NAW…NAW…the mo' I try to forget youuu, the mo' you hang on my MIIIINND!"* And Lord, Lord it seems to me that I see liquid pain just falling from her eyes. A liquid pain that hits the floor; a liquid pain that slides down her sequined dress, a liquid pain, that hits, swirls and shoots, like a water sprinkler.

And Christine looks up, and for one moment, one long moment, their eyes burn together, connect together. And Christine doesn't move it's as if she can't move. And without taking his eyes off of her….his power off of her, with one heavy gulp he downs his whiskey, gravels the empty glass on the table, with two heavy thuds, he squishes and squashes his cigarette into a near-by ash tray, Slaps a few bills on the table, and ups and leaves.

And Christine watches him with a frown on her face and fear in her eyes. She shoots up, slams down the mike, and mumbles something to Grady with pleading hands, and bucking eyes. And before he can answer that girl rumbles and stumbles her way through the crowd. And the crowd responds with a confused, "OOOOOOO…."

Grady shakes his head, sucks in his anger, mashes his lips, lifts up the neck of his guitar, and his fingers crash down onto that guitar justa hard. And a mad, screeching riff, a riff that reaches for the ceiling, a screech that stretches on and on and doesn't want to stop. And it's followed by a nagging, pestering groove. And that groove and that screech seem to gnarl, hiss and circle each other. And all the while Grady is watusi -ing his head and gnashing his teeth.

It's been three days now and ain't nobody seen nor heard song or note from Ms. Christine. Grady calls her house….nothing. Grady stops by her house and still….nothing. And the business is dwindling down to nothing. Because you see, Grady brings them in, but Christine keeps them in.

"Where's Christine…?" They all ask. We hunch up in our shoulders with blanks for faces and blanks for answers.

And on the fourth day two sets of wing tips walk in (plain clothes cops), with rumpled suits, and their flashing badges, flashing questions, flashing eyes and flashing holsters. They tell us that Christine was found dead at the nearby Grove Motel.

And that man….that man who ever he was did terrible, horrible things to that girl. Things I had never even heard of. Things I can not say, things I REFUSE to say. But I'll say this much, he wanted her alive while he did them. And I just KNOW, and you know that dollars to doughnuts, it was that man from the bar; the man she went running after that night. Lord, Lord, Lord, Christine thought she was chasing after cotton candy love that night, but she was only chasing after her death.

Oh, and I wonder as he was draining all the life out of that child, did he look into her eyes to see was he draining out all of her love too? Oh that's why I say, you've got to be so very careful going down life's road.

And they said he had duct taped her mouth, so what ever kind of torture he inflicted on her, couldn't nobody hear it….but God. But sometimes, late at night when I close my eyes I CAN hear her muffled screams. I CAN hear her muffled cries. And I pray to God, to have the good sense to watch out for life's swerves and curves.

Part X

Circa 1983

Oooh I tell you, I tell YOU… you might not believe it, but it sure is true! I'm the new singer here at the Blue Dahlia Night Club, right here on the south side of Chicago. Yes Honey, I've got me a grand old promotion. I've gone from bottle washer to a Blues caller and a note hauler. And I have a union card to prove it!

And just like it was when Christine was alive (the former singer), those blues pour outta my mouth every night, but I sure feel bad that the poor child had to die, after that child met with her demise, they had audition after audition, night after night, but Shady Grady was never satisfied. And then Mannie, that's the owner of the bar, reminds Grady that I was a Julliard drop-out. And Honey, that man took me under his mother-hen wing and pecked, clawed, and cawed my way into the Blues. And I have to tell ya that it fits me like spandex.

And we usually start the show with one of my favorite little numbers called, *"Scratch My Back,"* by the legendary Slim Harpo, founder of the "swamp blues" and Honey, if you KNOW anything about the blues, you know that man is talking about a helluva lot more than his back. Now, this song is usually done by a man, but Grady wants a woman's take on an old theme. And every night I make sure that my dress is waist cinching, curve fitting, and sho nuf side splitting.

And my favorite part of the song is at the beginning, when Grady slings back his guitar, and whips the harmonica from his shirt pocket. And then the drummer man counts off, and the moment I hear the wahs, wahs and wang, wangs of that harmonica, I put a frown on my face and throw my cheek to the side, like I've just been slapped by the Blues. And a mournful "OOOOOWWW," will tear from my throat. And the sho-nuf WAHS and the low-down WANGS hold me captive! And there ain't a thing I can do about it!

And I usually position myself on the far side of the stage, with the mike in my hand, but that sound, that beat, it summons me every time. It makes me spread out my hands in a 'T' formation (so they can be bound by the blues), I drop my head and I pop my fingers. And I get a criss-cross in my feet (so they can be chained by the blues) and with a hunch in, side my back I give in to my captors. And I surrender to my captors. And I wiggle on over to the WAHS and the WANGS. Grady spanks the side of that harmonica, like he's smacking on a race horse. And he cuts his eyes over at me, and takes a split of a breath from his harmonica and shouts, *"Come on over here Girl!"*

"I'm coming Daddy," I coo. *"I'm coming,"* And with a lick of his lips he'll conjure up my captors again. And when I hula and hooch on over to his side, I turn my back to him with a scowl on my face. And to me the music is sooo sleazy, sooo breezy, and down right ham hock greasy….And I use his body like a cat uses a scratching post, and I have to slide and glide down the side that man's waist, and thighs with my back bone. And I roll back my head and growl in a souped up whiskey voice, *"Awww you know I'm itching. And I don't know where to scratch. Come over here Baby and scratch myyyyy back!"* And the grinding, whining, and wheezing of his harmonica will command me to glide and slide back up his "scratching post" once again, like the Blues is a itching and a pinching at my back. And the tip-toeing, teasing funk of the bass guitar will creep on in.

And usually, at most bars the crowd doesn't get up until they're all drunk up, but Honey when the swamp blues come to calling they gotta answer. They let their bodies drift on down to that Bijou beat. And they wade in those murky waters, and they gotta shonuf dog paddle in those same murky waters (dance), because that's the power of the low-down, funk-down, dirty swamp blues! The crowd becomes a fever of voices, chants and demands. And I ride and I feed on this fever. A gravelly man's voice shouts. "Ahh shake it Mama, shake it like a cake mixer!"

And I hear a husky woman's voice near the front of the stage holler, "Sing it Annie Mae…sing yo song Girrrl!" And without even looking I just know its Big Mama Mozelle.

Big Mama Mozelle is one of the regulars at the bar. I love watching her in-between my sets. And she's a mighty big ole sumptin, and as tall as a tree, but Baby, she's built from the ground up. And ya talk about solid; her body is as solid as a blue chip stock! And Honey, when the Blues hit her, they hit her hard. She chicken wobbles her neck, tucks in her mouth, puts her hands on her hips (and ya better give her some room) and her body goes allll the waaay downtown (to the floor). And she doesn't bother to bring it back up either, she'll stay her behind right down there, for a long time, and she'll let her bottom thang swish around like the bristles on a car wash. And her back side looks like the curves on a shapely vase.

And after about a month or two of my singing stint, she catches me in between sets and struts her stuff over to my table. And her voice is as big and booming as she is, and she gives me a heavy-handed pat me on my shoulder and says, "Girrrl you know you be doing yo sho nuf thang up there on that stage. Every time you sing I get goose pimples." And all I can do is cut my eyes at Grady and look down at the floor. Because all the time I've been singing he's never complimented me. Sometimes, the other band members will slur out a nice remark. But Grady never parts his lips.

"Anyway," she says, "I'm giving a little after party tonight, and it sho wouldn't be NOTHING without you and the band there. 'Cause girl, you're hellyifying, and I just know you're coming."

And I shake my head, with tired, droopy dog eyes, and say, "I ain't coming nowhere tonight, but to my bed. Thanks, for the offer, but I just can't do it," and I twirl my drink around the table.

"Girrrl, I ain't taking no for an answer. Now I know where you live. Don't make me have to come up there and caveman yo ass down them stairs. 'Cause I will do it, tell her Grady?" Grady, who is sitting at the same table, with a bottle of beer to his lips, slams the brown bottle to the table. And he tightens his lips together, and a big smile zooms across his face, and he's barely able to hold the froth in his mouth. And he says, "Listen up Annie Mae, a word to the wise, I've seen it happen. If Big Mozelle wants ya, she'll come and get ya. I seen her handle a many men, right up here in this bar that way, she don't play."

And Big Mama crosses her arms, and her looming eyes and looming figure stares down at me, and says, "Hmmm, hmmm, now how you want this, the easy way, or Big Mo way? It makes me no never mind."

I wave a tired hand at her and nod my head, at that Amazon Queen. "Alright then, that's what I thought. Grady knows where I stay. He'll get ya there," she says, backing away, into the crowd.

There are hip-to-hip people at the after set, justa standing around with drinks in their hands, and chit-chatting their heads. And almost everybody from the bar seems to have made their way to Big Mozelle's apartment. And the place is well-lit. And I'm glad too, that way I can sho-nuf see what's in front of me. And if I look hard enough, what's in back of me, too. Me and Grady manage to get here early enough to cop a couch seat in the corner of the living room. And the music is playing, and Big Mozelle's voice is bellowing. "Hey, move it! Can't you see I'm trying to get by? SHIIIIIT!" She bumps and thumps her way over to us with some cocaine on a tray. Y'all better sniff up. This party is waay too dull for my standards. Let's get it rocking up in heah!"

"This is especially for y'all," Big Mozelle says, sitting down a shiny blue tray with three white mounds and a rolled up bill on it. And Big Mo does something I find strange; she slips Grady a special little wink and a smile. And I frown up my face trying to catch hold of the meaning.

And a second later I pay neither of the signals no mind, I'm ready to dig in Honey. Big Mozelle can't sit that stuff down fast enough. And before you can say, "Rick James" I'm digging in. I catch a frown on Grady's face outta the corner of my eye. "Girrrl, what you think you doing," he says.

"What it look like I'm doing, chantin Zen?" I shoot right back, and I'm justa a sniffing and a twitching.

"That ain't no blow girl, that's China White," Grady says, looking at me all gawk eyed.

And what did he say that for? "What…What?" I say, trying to focus. And I drop that dollar bill like its tainted. And I blink my eyes several times, and can't see nothing, all I see are flashing, white lights justa blinking and a flickering. And I feel a tingling shooting up my nose. And my hands fly out in from of me, like I'm trying to chase away the brightness and I'm justa blinking my behind off…and my mouth hits the floor, my feet hits the floor and my inhibition…Honey, my inhibition sho-nuf hits the floor. And before I know it I hear some fool holler, "WHHHOOOOH…GAWDDD DAMN!" And I ain't got sense enough to realize that the fool is me!

And there hasn't been a word invented yet for how good this sistah is feeling. And I'm ready now; I'm ready to take on the CIA aaannd the KGB (Bring all their asses on!). And I'm standing here with my hands on my hips, smacking my lips and justa a snapping my finger tips. And I say to the large party crowd, "Alright all y'all

Motha Fuckas, which one of y'all got some works (heroin works)? I know somebody up in this Motha fucka got some works!" I shout again with my body justa a snaking and a quaking. And I feel a tug at my arm, and Grady says, "Sit your crazy ass down," And I jerk my arm away from that man, like he's got a disease or something. And everybody standing up with their drinks in hand frown at me, stop action…freeze frame…eyes blaring…face staring.

"Annie Mae, sit your ass down, you're making a fool of yourself," Grady says, this time yanking at my arm.

And I snatch myself away from that man as hard as I can, and I spit out, "Get yo hands off me, you don't know me like that!"

And I hear Big Mozelle, hot footing her way towards me, "'Scuse me…scuse me…" she says, trying to fight her way through the crowd. She towers all over me, looking me all down and up, twisting her face all up, talking about, "What the fuck's yo problem?"

"I want me some works…BIIITCH!" I say with my arms swaying. And a "OOOH," groans throughout the crowd. Because nobody…but nobody in their right mind ever calls Big Mozelle a Bitch. She's old school Baby, she doesn't play that. She'll put her shoe so far up your behind, you'll be spitting out the label, but I ain't worried about a thing, because I'm full of my warrior powder. Her eyes get as big as saucers, and she flinches, like I'm splattering hot grease in her face. She paint brushes the crowd with crocodile eyes, and slowly strokes me with those same eyes.

"Sit down Annie Mae, you've had enough," pleads Grady now, standing by my side.

And I ain't worried about no Big Mozelle or no nothing else! Besides, she likes having musicians at her party. It's good for her image and the party too…hell.

Big Mozelle has her hand on her hips, and a twist on her lips, she looks at me slowly nodding her head, and saying, "Hmmm…Hmmm…(like she's sizing me up) you're sure that's what you want Annie Mae, 'cause it seems to me like you're already full."

"SHIIIT…that was just an appetizer, I'm ready for the main course," I say, scratching my nose and with my body bending like a palm tree.

And Big Mozelle is still twisting her mouth; she taps her foot on the floor, and says "Alright, I'll be right back." And she makes her way through the still silent crowd. And to this day, I don't know if Big Mozelle says alright because she wants to appease me…or because I called her a Bitch. And for the first time I realize that since

I stood up and started acting a fool, there hasn't been any music playing. And I sit down, and Grady joins me, "Annie, what the fuck you doing?" he hisses.

"Something I should of done a long time ago," I say, and I can feel my heart justa racing, and I'm not sure if it's racing because of the China White, or because of what I'm about to do to myself.

Big Mozelle struggles her way back through the crowd, she's back in no time. And all the while she's staring at me something fierce. "Here ya go," she says, setting a black leather pouch on the table.

"Where you get this shit from, Big Mozelle," Grady says, looking up at her and back down at the pouch.

"I use to be into it real heavy. It liked to have taken me right on up outta here," Big Mozelle says, not taking her eyes off of me. It's as if her eyes are hand stitched to my eyes. She raises up her hands, her bell bottom sleeves fold back and for the first time I realize that they're swollen to the size of oven mitts. This is the gift that Lady Heroin gave me. And if you're not strong enough, not careful enough she'll leave you a gift too…Annie Mae." And I want that woman to unstitch her eyes off me. And she finally looks down at the bag, and with a smack of her lips she says, "I like having it around. It reminds me that I made it through the storm." And with her end finger she slides the black pouch closer to me and says, "Here, knock yourself out." I look down at that black pouch and up again, but this time Big Mama is gone.

"Annie Mae, I don't know what you're trying to prove, but this sure ain't worth it Baby Girl," Grady says, narrowing his eyes and shaking his head. "I might snort the shit every now and then…but I ain't NEVAH went down that road. Ugh..ugh, I've seen too many fallen soldiers to do that shit.'

And I click off the Grady channel. And I see his mouth justa flapping, but he ain't saying nothing I want to hear, so I just concentrate on that white powder instead. And I finally see his mouth has stopped moving, and I say, "Can you do it for me Grady? I know you know how?"

And that man pulls back his neck and cocks his head, and says, "BABY GIRRRL! Did you hear anything I just said…DID YOU?"

And I just slump back in the couch. I don't say nothing, and he doesn't either. And…"FINE," I snap "I'll do it my damn self. I don't need you no how." I say, and I start fishing around in that little black pouch, smacking the syringe, and the cooking spoon down on the table.

"Wait Annie Mae, you don't know what you're doing," he says, covering my hand with his. "Don't go down this street, Annie, it's a dead end. I know Baby Girl…I told you my own mama was a hard-core junkie…don't go down this street…it ain't no coming back."

"I been down a many dead end streets before," I say, snatching away my hand. And I strain my eyes and soften my voice and say, "For the first time I feel soo alive Grady, I ain't never felt this alive before. I feel like I'm not afraid of nothing or nobody."

"Then sit back and groove with that feeling Baby Girl, let it be enough. You're my prize singer, I swear I don't want to lose you," he says shaking his head. "I lost my Mama because of this shit… And I lost Christine…I don't wanna lose you too."

"You ain't gonna lose me… it's just that it feels so good, it feels so right. I ain't gonna get strung out or nothing." I say.

"Shiiiit, you already talking like a junkie, girl, and you don't even know it," he says shaking his head and waving his hand.

I take his hand and I say, "I ain't gone let no lil' powder ruin what I have with you Grady, it means the world to me, but at the same time just this ONCE I need you to let me have this Grady…PLEEZE. I need to know this feeling. I ain't gonna never let YOU down, you mean too much to me," I say squeezing on his hand.

I've been waiting all my life to see a miracle and I ain't seen one yet Baby Girl, and I know I ain't gonna see one now. My mama would have me doing some crazy stuff just so she could cop. Stuff I'm still ashamed of to this day. Sometimes, she'd force me to give her the injections." He says, shaking his head, biting down on his lip. And he looks at the syringe for what seems like a long time. And my heart is racing again. He grips my hand and he squeezes it so hard, so hard I can't feel it anymore. "Promise me Annie Mae; promise me you ain't gone be no fallen soldier. Promise ME you're gone be MY miracle and not let this stuff rule you, promise me Annie? I'm hoping and praying for a piece of that miracle Baby Girl"

"I promise," I say…real quiet like.

"I ain't no fool Annie Mae," he says, but heeey, it's your life…your veins," and with a defeated drop of his shoulders and a shake of his head he digs into his pocket for a lighter. And I watch him cook that stuff up, take that syringe and draw that stuff up. And

Lord, Lord why don't I run Jesus…why don't I just tell Grady I don't want it anymore…WHY?

And he ties a rubber band around my upper arm, as tight as he can make it, and I stare at that man, and he stares me right back, and he winces and with a strong, "HUMMP," he gives that rubber one last, hard yank. "You still want this," he asks, lifting up that needle, popping on that needle. And I close my eyes and give him a quick nod.

He slides that needle into my arm real easy like, and I just feel a little bit of a stinging pinch…that's all. And I look down at the blood rushing up into the syringe, and it mingles with that clear liquid. And he takes the plunger and he pushes it down again and there's nothing in that syringe, and then he brings the plunger back up again, "Stop teasing me," I say. And my blood…my life, shoots up and the clear liquid shoots up, and my life, my blood and that liquid court each other and kiss each other and mate with each other (right there in that syringe)…and he pushes the syringe down…all the way down, one… last…time. And it never comes back up again.

And I see now, that the needle, it ain't no needle at all, it's a bill…a bill I'll NEVER stop paying for. And that liquid, it ain't no liquid at all, it's a journey, a journey that I'll never return from. And I bang my head against the wall; And I hear a booming in my head that's so loud, so loud I raise my head back up and I crash it right back into the wall. You see my inner clock is going off…DONNNG…DONNNG…its now hell o'clock do you know where your innocence has gone?!

And I close my eyes and I lift and seep inside myself, and I see my inner self, and there are patches of colors down here, light colors, bright colors, iridescent colors, shimmering colors, odd colors, and unknown colors…life colors zooming all inside my body. And I jump on one of those patches of colors and I surf, I ride, I glide and I slide along the gushing waves of my blood stream. In and out down and up, I'm riding high on my patches of colors, my patches of life…But I see something inside of myself, something dark, booming and angry, something that's trying to push its way up outta me. And I'm scared.

And out of fear I open my eyes and I catch a glint of sadness in Grady's eyes, a glint that darts and shifts in and out and back again. And my eyes move down to his mouth, and I'm amazed at the pinkness of his mouth, the fullness of his mouth, the shape of his mouth. And I take my hand and my fingers and I let them see and saw all across that mouth, all across his mustache, and they see and saw all across his eyelids, neck, throat and chest. And I pull myself closer to that man, and his warm breath lingers and plays against my skin. And the scent of his breath is like a ribbon of cigarettes, whiskey and hard times, lots of hard time.

And I take his hand and I guide his hands to places that hadn't wanted a man, or needed a man in a long, long time. I guide his hands and sweep his hands all across my mountains, my hills and my valleys, hungry places that need him to vacation there, places where I want his hands to be, places his hands also want to be.

And I curl my fingers up inside his curly hair, and I press his mouth hard against mine, deep inside of mine. And our tongues are flicking and clicking, speaking a language only they seem to understand. And I let my mouth offer him things; it offers him all my pain, all my disappointments, and all of my suffering. And his mouth becomes my first aid. His mouth puts an ace bandage around my pain. And his fingers alcohol rubs my disappointments and iodine's all of my suffering. Right here on this couch…right here in front of every body (where's my shame?). And I don't know it yet, but they are all bearing witness this night, and they are all able to bear testimony to my destruction, my downfall. And I catch a snatch of something, something outta the corner of my eye. I see Big Mozelle with her folding arms, narrow eyes, justa smiling, justa smiling.

Chapter XI

"**WAKE UP**," orders my dream voice.

"Wha…" I say, waking up startled, and I 'm blinking eyes, fumbling hands and stumbling fingers I'm patting for two loves, my warrior powder (heroin), it's right there on the night stand, in the small plastic bag just where I left it and then my Baby, but nothing is there to greet me, but a cold, lumped up sheet. And my whole body flies into a panic. I jump up out of that bed, wiggle into my robe and race from room to room, and from pillar to post, just looking for MY Baby.

I find him there at the kitchen table, with the early morning light on the side of his face. He's having his usual breakfast of misfits, black coffee and a cigarette. And I relax my relief, but something in the way that he's fully dressed, with his coat on at six o'clock in the morning stirs and unsettles me.

He takes a deep pull on that cigarette, and looks over at me with narrow eyes. "You're up awfully early," I say, knotting my robe together and pulling up a nearby chair. And the chair squeals and alarms across the floor, and there's something inside of me that wants to squeal out too (but I don't know why).

"Yeah," he says, scraping his fingers through his hair. "I'm getting ready to roll." He takes another pull on the cigarette. And I look up at the gray pools of smoke, swirling and then shrinking into nothing.

I nod my head and finger a nearby napkin holder that sits in the middle of the table. "Oh, you'll be back later on huh?" I ask (afraid of the answer).

He takes in a long sip of coffee, and it sounds like a child blowing gurgling through a straw. He slams his cup down, like he's slamming down judgement. And the sound rings of heartache. "Nah, I ain't coming back Annie Mae," he says, slowly twisting his cigarette butt into the plastic ashtray. "I ain't never coming back." Now God knows I'm old enough and should be strong enough to have grown some extra gristle on my back bone, from all the other times I have drunk from this well of disappointment, but his words sting and jab, jab and sting and before I know it, tears start tumbling down my cheeks. And my arms reach for his chest, but he pulls me away…they reach for his waist, he pulls ME away!

"I thought you loved me," I ask, with frowns of confusion on my face. "YOU told MEEE you loved me," I say still reaching for his waist.

"Oh I do," he says, scooting back from the table and standing up. "But it's hard to love a woman that's a junkie." My hand bangs against my mouth as if I touched something hot. "What did you say?" I ask, heaving on the truth. "What did you say, dammit?"

"You're a junkie Annie Mae, we both know it," he says, shaking his head and pursing his lips. "I tried Annie Mae, tried to ride that hope train right along with you Baby. And all the while I knew the train was gonna jump the tracks. But I still rode it with ya Baby…I can't ride it anymore Annie Mae. You're going down. And I'm not going down with you," he says with a twist for a mouth and scissors for hands (scissors that slice through me and the air).

I scamper from the chair with the taste of snot in my mouth, and tears in my eyes. "But you said we could work it out. You said it would be alright, and if you want me off the shit, I'm off…I swear on everything I know and love, I'm OFF!" I say, with air gashing hands.

"You've been singing that same song for six months Annie Mae. It's been six long months girl and you're strung out like a clothes line. I told you Annie Mae, I told yooouuu that my mama was a junkie, she O.D. on that shit. She lay up in some abandoned building with a needle sticking out of her arm for THREE whole days, being a snack for the rats and the flies. And I'll be damn straight to hell before I go through that shit again. I was a child then Annie Mae, I didn't have a choice…I didn't have a choice." And his eyes flutter and his lips sputter on a piece of pain. "If it ain't alright by now, it's not gonna be alright. And he cocks his head and says, "What you think Annie Mae, you honestly think can get over that shit the way you would a cold? Hmmp, I'm outta here. I'll send for my clothes later," he says, heading for the door. "I'm sorry," he whispers.

"Sorry….Sorry," I scream, "Will sorry keep you here?"

I dart past him and slide towards the door, with my dignity thrown on the floor and I get down on my knees…on MY knees, begging that man to stay.

"But you said we could work it out. You said it would be alright". I say in a scared voice.

Grady stops cold in his tracks, raises the corner of his mouth and looks down at me as if I'm a hot piece of nothing. "Annie Mae get up, get out of my way". He says. My lips starts quivering and my hands shake in front of my chest. "I'll do anything you say Baby…anything, but please, please don't leave me". "You're all I know", I plead.

I'm only human, Annie Mae. I'm only human", he says shaking his head, and patting his hands against the air. "Now, for the last time, get the fuck out of my way!" Grady says, with warning signs flashing in his eyes.

And before I know it, my hands leap for his leg, snatch for his leg, he tries to shake me off, wiggle me off, but I ain't coming off…I ain't coming off ! And every time he shakes me, my tears shake, snake and fling across the floor. Grady takes his hands and tries to pry my fingers away. But you see, every time he tries my fingers just pry deeper into his pants leg.

"You crazy ass bitch, get the fuck off me", he shouts trying to wedge the door open, and shake me off at the same time.

All I have left of him is his pants leg, and Lord knows I can't let go of that….I just can't let go. Then with a gravelly roar from his chest, he leans over and grabs the door knob with both hands and whacks the door against my spine as hard as he can, so hard that I arch my back from the pain. Sensing that he has the upper hand, he whacks, and whacks, and keeps on whacking. "I love you baby. I love you". I scream between the whacks. "I love you". It's almost as if he's trying to exorcize that love right out of me with every whack.

Then there's a long string of silence. The only thing that's heard in that room is our breaths, rising to meet each other and falling away from each other. He looks down at me. I look up at him. Again that look…that look that says I'm a hot piece of nothing, smears across his face. And he heaves and pants and pants and heaves. His mouth becomes a cloud of anger; a cloud that blooms and bursts into snarling teeth, protruding teeth, bulldog teeth. He slinks around the opening of the door with me still holding on and clinging on.

He slides my body across the dusty hallway floor. And my knees and breast scrape and rake across the dark floor boards. "I ain't letting go Grady….You hear me, I ain't letting go". I growl, clinging tighter to his pants leg.

Then Grady stops for a flash of a second and smiles down at me at the top of the stairwell…and BOOM…he jerks my behind down those stairs. Grady takes me on a hell ride… a hell ride I won't soon forget.

Boom… Boom… Boom… my body sputters down the stairs. My body folds and slumps over the stairs and splinters of shame and dust pop into my open mouth. I spit them out, but still I hold on. I hold on like a Sanctified Lady, to the prayer book…I hold on!

Then half way down the stairs Shady Grady stops. He's huffing and puffing and I'm huffing and puffing. And I think I have won. My baby is gonna stay…My baby is… Boom! He lifts both hands to the banister and jumps up and kicks and flicks. And I look down at my two hands and there ain't nothing there. Nothing there but pain, grief and defeat…defeat. And I heave in a breath, a breath so hard and so long it turns into a howl. A howl so loud and so strange I don't even recognize it as mine. And Grady is grinning back at me and hop-scotches his way out the door. But not before I unscrew the already loose wooden ball from the bottom of the stair case and lamb it dead-straight at his head. POP…it jumps from his head and lands in the doorway and roles slightly…back and forward…forward and back.

Ooh I tell you that man stands cold-still in that doorway, with the icy, autumn wind justa flapping at his thin coat. And I can feel the coldness licking at my half clothed body.

And that man takes his hand and rubs the back of his head and he looks at his hand searching for blood, but there's nothing there. And his body trembles for a minute and he turns around real slow like. And I can't see nothing, nothing but his eyes. They're as wide as tablespoons. And a cold, gray ghost of anger pours from his mouth climbs and floats up the stairs and settles at my feet.

And I can't feel nothing, but a hot slap of fear. And still I have the gumption to sit there and let my mouth curl and twist on my sassiness and I shake my head on my sassiness, and I say, "You ain't shit…you ain't never been shit. You need me, I ain't nevah needed yoou! Go back to your shit-hole and wallow in it!"

Before I know it, that man darts up the stairs and lunges at me and I shake now, I shake like palsy. His cigarette breath coats my face. He pulls back his head and tightens his face, tightens his eyes and tightens his jaw (and for a moment his eyes and mouth blink and twitch and twitch and blink). And he snatches in a deep breath of something, something so deep it rises his shoulders, and releases his shoulders and with almost loving hands he cups my chin, strokes my hair, plays with my eyebrows and my cheeks, and says, "If you wanna hurt yourself Baby girl, fine, strap on your womanhood and gone and do what you feel you gotta do, that's your bizness. But don't think for one minute that I'm gonna do it for ya…that just ain't my way. Learn to be good to yourself Annie Mae, learn to love yourself." He says, and his cold lips peck me on the cheek….His words…love yourself, seem to scour and scrape, scrape and scour at my skin, like Dutch cleanser…love yourself. I squeeze my eyes shut trying to chase those words away, swish those words away. And a minute later I open my eyes and he's gone…just like that he's gone, without a creak in the floorboards, or a rustle of his clothing…he's gone.

I sit there, watching the snowflakes blow, circle and push around the wooden ball in the open doorway, and I let the cold air stir and sweep across my body. I sit there, waiting for the storm to come.

Part XII

Lord, Lord, Lord, did I ever tell you about No-Neck Johnson? He works at the Blue Dahlia, same as I do, except he's a bouncer. And Baby, ya wanna talk about ug—layyyy. And I may be as wrong as a gorilla in a tiara and a tu-tu, but it seems to me, when the Good Lord got ready to make No-Neck Johnson, He musta run fresh out of bone, and I think he ran over to ugmo depot and got some cinder blocks and used them instead. And I think that the Good Lord was in a playful mood on this particular day. And he stuffs those cinder blocks, skin, eyes, nose and everything else into this big bag you see? And he doesn't tie that bag or nothing. He just takes it and closes his eyes and swings it around and around with His mighty hands. And He twirls and whirls that bag… VROOM…VROOM…VROOM! And with one powerful hurl, He throws that bag as far as He can. And when that bag lands so does all of No- Neck, and the Good Lord gives No-Neck the once over. And with a deep sigh, He tries several times to make some since of this mess, called No-Neck, but each time No-Neck would slump back over, with one eye going this way the other eye going that way, his nose going the wrong way and No-Neck's mouth going every which way, and eventually He shakes His head, throws up His hands, and said, "Hey, forget about it," and He calls it a day.

And like I said, that child is so ugly; his mama has to feed him with a sling-shot (I ain't lying)! And Baby, he ain't got neck the first! In the back of his head where his neck should be, it's a staircase I tell ya, a staircase of flab (if that staircase was any lower you'd trip on it). And in the front ain't nothing there either, nothing but a head and shoulders (I ain't lying). Child, that man has a definite case of the three B's (big, black and burly). He musta weigh a good 350. And he likes to stand outside of the bar popping peppermints into his mouth. And not one at a time, oh noo, not Mr. No-Neck, we're talking four or five. And then if you get close enough to him, you can hear him rolling them around in his big, greasy mouth and justa a smacking them down and crunching them down all night long.

One night, it seems like that very No-Neck is my only friend in the world. Me and Grady have just broken up, and it's so hard to perform on stage with that man, sing love songs with that man, stare into the eyes of that man, knowing that I can never again have that man. And it seems that the only way I can get on that stage every night is with a good dose of my warrior powder.

Sometimes, when I leave the club it's all I can do to prop myself against a building and watch him drive away. And every time it feels as if a piece of me is driving away too. And it seems as if No-Neck catches a whiff of my sadness, and I musta looked an awfully, miserable mess because one night he comes up behind me and places his catcher's mitt like hands on my shoulders and says, "If ya need anything Annie Mae I'm here for ya…Do you heah me…anything."

And what did that ugmo say that for? Chile, my mind starts to rolling, squeezing and playing on those words, like they're silly putty. "I'm here for ya." I don't know about YOU, but those aren't words I get to hear every day. And sometimes thinking back on it now, I feel sorta bad about the whole ordeal. That man was offering me his friendship, but all I wanted was play ship. And you know I never even think enough of that man to find out his real name. That's one more thing I have to add to MY Rolodex of regrets. But you see, I can't help it, because let me tell you something …something that I KNOW,I ain't only putting this warrior powder into my veins I'm injecting street smarts too. And that's something I ain't never had before. And these street smarts teach me how to radar in on a person's weakness, and then prey on pounce on that weakness….and it's easy to me (too easy).

And I ain't gonna lie to ya, life is already hard, we all know that, but when you have a a drug habit to boot, seems like every corner you look in, life becomes a boxing match, doing a Joe Frasier on yo stomach. And oh, I've done things for these drugs, things I ain't too proud of. Just a short-while ago I remember looking down on people standing on a corner fiening and weaning from this dope mess. They're all doubled over in pain, and their lives are sho-nuf doubled over in pain…and sometimes if you look at them too long, their eyes will stare up at you and beg out to you. And yet I have ALLOWED this to happen to ME…CHOSE this to happen to me! Oh I tell you, I tell you, sometimes I'd rather stick a knife in my chest than to stick another needle in my veins. But I bet you everything I know and love, that the minute I stick that needle in my vein…I venture to that land of no regrets.

Sometimes, when I cook up my warrior powder, and I watch it bubble up, and soup up on my spoon, I can't help but to wonder…Is my future as black as this spoon? And if you look hard enough, just beneath the caked on tar you'll see my dreams…dreams that are now peeling scabs and unhealed needle marks.

Me and No-neck start hanging out. We score drugs together, drink together, take out our problems and examine them together. And I just know it's a matter a time before I pop the magic question on him, but I sure didn't think it would be so soon. And one night after work I get up enough gumption to ask that man to loan me a $100.00. And you ain't got to be no-kind of Sigmund frigging Freud to see that No-Neck has an Annie Mae Jones. And now you know as well as I do that I intend to pay that man back, like I intend to smooch with the Seven Dwarfs! Living a junkie life you cash in a whole lotta things…see? But one thing you should never cash in is your conscience and mine went up for sale a long time ago

And I just know that if it wasn't for this drug mess that I would never fix my mouth to ask that man for nothing like that. And do you know that No-Neck smiles a little smile, and digs into his pocket (just like that) and fans it out to me…to me…an itching, scratching junkie. And I smile politely, and I hand him a thank you politely, and I cram that money deep into my bosom. And all the while I' m thinking this man must be a Stone Age kinda fool, because they sho don't make 'em like this anymore.

And after about a month or so No-Neck starts getting a little bit frantic about his money, hounding me, stalking me down for his lil' $100.00. And now come-on with the come-on what self-respecting junkie pays their debts? That's what I wanna know.

And sure enough after work I start playing in-cog-negroe with that N0-Neck, and I play dodge fool with that man too. After work I high –tail my behind upstairs to my apartment. One night after work this cute lil' white boy is interviewing me for the *"READER",* (a local newspaper). And I'm sitting at the now-closed up bar, sipping on my drink and sipping on the questions this reporter is asking me (and you know that all the while I'm thumbing and rubbing the heroin that's inside my skirt pocket…my warrior powder Honey). Mannie the bar owner trusts me enough to lock up everything (I know if he keeps trusting me in time there won't be anything to lock up…because I would have taken it all). Right now, I can't wait to get my behind upstairs, so I can click the electric fan on, put some Billie Holiday on, and get my sho-nuf nod on.

And you know I open up the front door to my apartment and its dark in there just the way I left if. And…a catcher's mitt like hands cup my face and mouth. And his hot, peppermint smelling breath is slapping at my cheek and I know…I just know that it's No-Neck coming to collect his due! And I try and scream and breathe through those catcher's mitt hands, but I can't seem to do either. The only thing that's coming out of my mouth is a muffled groan. And he seems so big towering in back of me. "Yeah…yeah… you remember me now don't cha…ugh? All this time you forgot who I was didn't ya? Yeah…yeah (And I shake my head something fierce trying to tell him I didn't forget who he was). Run now BITCH, let me see you run now," he says. And the word bitch is lathered with spit and hatred. "Yeah, ug huh since yo ass started singing you think you hot shit now don't ya…Ugh?" he says shaking me. "But you ain't SHIT, but a junkie ass bitch! Do you think I'm gone let you do me wrong …huh…huh?" he says clamping his hands tighter around my neck.

"Ya got that fo' me…huh…huh? Ya got my money huh…junkie ass Bitch…Ya got MYY money?" I nod my head signaling I Do have it (this fool is gonna hurt me..maybe even KILL me for a $100.00? That's all my life means to him is a $100.00…that's all?). And Lord knows I barely have two pieces of hope to rub together, but I got to get loose from No-Neck. And he shakes my head and my throat with his catcher's mitt hands. "Ya lying ass Bitch…ya ain't got shit. Ahh, but I got sumptin' for you! I'm gonna have fun taking it outtta yo ass. You wanna use me up just like those other girls….Don't cha, around heah shaking yo tits at me…wiggling yo ass at me. Ahh but No-Neck got sumptin' for ALL y'all asses. YOU ain't NOTHIN' (And he rattles my head) NOTHIN' but another hoish ass bitch I've GOTTA HURT!...You gone learn some respect for NO-NECK do YOU heah ME," he says shaking my head (and I try to nod the best I can)…. "But I ain't gotta hurt you, 'cause we gone be friends ain't we…Annie Mae…good friends…yeah," he says, digging his tongue into my ear and twisting my breast. And he starts dragging me towards my living room couch. And I know Jesus if I do something it's got to be…NOW! And I let my fingers do the talking; I wring on that man's mountain oysters, like I'm wringing out laundry. And that man snatches his hands away from my breast and neck like I set them ablaze. And he grabs hold of his manhood justa bending and screaming like a 10 year old. And I run for that door, and I grapple that door, and I open up that door. And I hurry up and grab hold of the other side of that door. And I feel his hand yanking at my hair, trying to yank me back into that hell room. And I yell, "CALL THE POLICE!! CALL THE--". And I can feel his hand pulling and tearing at my head, but you see I hold on to that knob…I hold on to that knob, like it's a life boat. I hold on so hard I can feel it snapping and breaking on the inside. And I scream, I scream like it's going out of style. And a angry looking man with nothing on but his tee-shirt and underwear, opens his door. And I know No-Neck won't dare show his face in that hallway. So I take full advantage. And Lord I'm justa screaming and a jerking like a crazy woman. "CALL THE POL…" I try to scream. He yanks me by my hair again, he yanks me by my head so hard it feels like nails are being pulled outta my scalp. And he yanks me back into that hell room.

And Lord I just know that No-Neck is mad now, but you see I'm mad too. He takes my head and shoves me down to the floor face first. And he kicks the door close with his foot so hard it makes a BOOM sound…and when I hear that BOOM…I'm not mad anymore, see? I'm just scared. And I can hear his free hand clinking at his belt buckle. And my hands are feeling around in the dark because I know I got a small table around here somewhere. And I have a present for No-Neck waiting on that table. And I sho-do find what I'm looking for. And I'm gonna deliver it B.U.P. (bleed upon delivery). You see I reach for my old fashioned, heavy, black phone. And I smother the receiver under my chest. And that fool does just what I want him to. He takes my ankles and flips me over like I'm a pancake. And SURPRISE I bend up and lam and slam that receiver right up side that fool's head. And…POW …POW...! I pound on that man's head, like Julia Child pounds on steak. "YOUUU Ho-ish Bitch," he screams, "You ho-ish ass BITCH!" And we're really tussling now and I'm trying to stand, because I know he's really going to hurt me, but every time I do, he slaps me down with his weight. And Lord, Lord, that man snatches that phone from my hand and smacks it in MY face. He slaps me so hard… I can hear breaking and snapping, and I feel it ALL…just letting go, my blood, my grit, and my teeth, my life…letting go smashing and crashing into my mouth. And my face rolls over in a slow motion, lagging kinda pain.

"Ahh ya like it rough don't ya BITCH? Ya wanna play rough…UGH? Come on lets play rough," he says, placing his heavy knee upon my neck. And I can feel my wind pipe burning and begging … And I can't breathe Jesus…I can't breathe anymore. And I'm afraid of choking on all that blood and gook that's already inside of my mouth. So as best I can, I take all the breath I can squeeze up and I spit up all my teeth, blood, and grit, onto that man's legs. And I just want to breathe, that's all…And my hands are waving and clawing at No-Neck's thigh.

"LET ME BREATHE!" I wanna scream. " GAWDDAMMIT LET ME BREATHE!"

I'm trying my best to get him up off of me, but there's a part of me that doesn't want to breathe anymore. See? It just wants to slip away "Ugh…Ugh I'm gone fix yo ass, YOU gone learn some respect." And No-Neck ain't satisfied with just that one knee on my neck he pushes his other knee down on my chest, while he's fishing around in his pockets trying to find something And I can feel a crushing and a popping in my chest, and then a pressure I ain't never felt before…it's my lungs…there going flat, flat as pizza dough. And my eyes …my eyes… try to stay focus on what few little pieces of light I can find, but there starting to let me down too…and that same part of me that doesn't want to breathe anymore…it doesn't want to see anymore either. And I catch a glint of brightness shining from No-Neck's fist. And I see it coming towards my head…I want to move my head, but I can't (and the more I struggle, the more I can't breathe) He crashes his fist into the side of my head. And a white bag of pain wraps itself around my head so tight, it sucks away at my scalp and then chews its way inside my skull, crunching its way into a side of my brains…and my brains smash and tear into the other side of my skull. And my skull pushes into my scalp, my scalp expands and explodes and my blood gushes and sputters unto the floor.

Something else slips out of that open wound, something that ain't suppose to slip out. Meeee! Slipping outta myself is as easy as slipping out of a dress. And I don't see nothing much in that dark, I look over at what seems to be my body but it look like a bundle of old clothes, but it seems like I hear the tearing and the popping of those clothes. And I hear No-Neck saying, "You're one dead Bitch now, you're one dead Bitch," over and over again. And my rag doll body is just laying there ain't saying nothing, ain't doing nothing. And I guess No-Neck knows it's something wrong, and he slaps my face: WHOPP!…but I can't feel it see? And he says, "Don't you pass out on ME. I want you to enjoy allll of THIS!"

But it's too late, I ain't got time to stay, I can't stay if I want to, because something is yanking at me, and jerking at me, pulling me down into the darkness of that room (a darkness I never knew before). And I'm zooming down into that darkness, a darkness that leads to cold murky waters. And I can taste that dirty water in my mouth seems like. And something is still pulling at me…jerking at me, it won't let me go. And I'm being snatched from those murky waters and I'm drip-dried and placed here on this flimsy bridge. And this bridge is nothing, nothing but rope and plank. And it's shaking and a swaying like a hammock. And I grab hold to both sides as tight as I can. And I look beneath me back down into those dark, bubbling, oily looking waters with raging, foaming white caps. And the wind whips across my face, and it stings like a sand storm.

On the other side of the bridge is a dark, foggy, mist. And a voice comes outta that mist… a voice that brings about stillness (the bridge isn't swaying anymore, the waters aren't rushing anymore, and the wind isn't stinging anymore) a voice that's as black, as strong, and as down home as elderberry wine.

"Whyyyy should Iyyyyee be lonely? Whyyyyy should Iyyyye be discouraged, when GEEESUS issss my Potion. And Iyyye knowwww he watches over meeeee." And it seems like her voice fingers through my hair, eyebrows and face.

"Is that You Big Mama? Is that you?" I say.

"Is that my suga wooga over there? Is that my Baby Girl…Is that my Annie Mae?' the voice ask.

"Yes Big Mama it's me…its MEEE!" And the child in me leaps up, jumps up, and swells up and my feet want to leap up, but I'm too afraid of this rickety bridge. And I'm so anxious, so excited to see my Big Mama, I have to bite down hard on the side of my fist, just to contain myself.

"Hold on Chile, I'll be there directly," says the voice. And I hear her footsteps coming across the planks.

And out of that dark, foggy mist I see Big Mama, the one who was always on my side, Big Mama. Her hair is silver gray, shining so bright, I can barely look at it (almost aluminum foil bright), and her skin is dark, burnt pecan dark, and she's wearing a flowery house dress. And Big Mama isn't missing a leg anymore, she walks with both of them, but she ain't doing as much walking as she is floating. And I leap into Big Mama's arms, like a child leaps into Christmas. And Big Mama smells just like she use to, she smells of caramel cakes, the 4th of July and church picnics. And she cups my face and brings it up to her face, and Big Mama's hands are as warm and comforting as a pot of greens. And again the child in me swells up and it wants to tell her everything. "Ohhh, I miss you Big Mama and so much has happened."

"SHHHHH," she says placing her warm finger against my lips. "I know Chile…I know." And I see a sorrow in Big Mama's eyes…only there not Big Mama's eyes anymore. Big Mama's eyes were the color of strap molasses when she was alive, but these eyes are the color of dull dimes. "And there's sooo much more that's going to happen to you…Baby," Big Mama's says, and Big Mama sucks on her teeth, but it looks like she's chawing on old piece of bitter tobacco that she can't quite spit out.

My body stiffens like concrete, and I hold on to Big Mama's sleeves as tight as I can, and I say, "What you mean Big Mama? I ain't going back there no more. I'm staying…right here… with you."

"Nawww, you've GOT to go back Baby, yo place isn't here yet. You've got more learning and a WHOLE lot more earning to do, befo' you can find a place over heah," Big Mama says, caressing my cheek and justa smiling her knowing smile.

"I REFUSE to go back Big Mama…I refuse," I say, still yanking at her sleeves.

And Big Mama tilts back her head, purses her lips and her eyelids become dark, heavy curtains, and its like the future is draping over Big Mama's eyes…a future I can't see. And after a while she opens her eyes and says, "I know yo road ain't been easy Baby, and I sho ain't gone lie to ya, and tell ya it gets less bumpy, because it don't…but Baby at the end of yo road it's gonna smooth on out and all of those bumps are gonna roll out into a river bank of joy.

'Cause ya see Annie Mae, you're my beautiful Dandelion Baby. People might pluck at you, ahh they might pick at you, but they can't get to you, in the end you'll still be standing strong. They might wanna get you down, and wear you down, but they can't. It'll take a powerful piece of something to get MY Dandelion down…Your roots are too strong, and they run too, too deep for that. You's a fighter Baby, always have been, why Baby, when you came into the world you came out feet first, justa kicking, and yo legs and feet have been flitting and flaying every since." And Big Mama narrows her eyes and holds me close to her and says, "They can't stop you, My Dandelion Baby, they can't stop you."

And Big Mama squeezes me, she squeezes me soo hard, so tight, I swoon and it's all I can do to hold on to my Big Mama. And I feel something I ain't felt in a long, long time…Love… a make you weak in yo knees kinda love, a shelter from the rain kinda love…a stronger than any man's army kinda love …a forever kinda love.

BEEP…BEEP…BEEP… I feel PAIN, a 500 lb man sitting on my chest kinda pain. And I feel hands, so many hands, soft hands, rough hands, busy hands, lifting hands, doing things on my body at the same time hands. And I hear words, rushing words, strange words…like intubate (placing a tube down the throat)...flail chest (crushed and broken ribs)…subdural hematoma (bleeding on the brain) and…anal tears.

And I'm being rushed somewhere and I'm being carried there so fast that the breeze is flapping over my skin and wringing out my hair. And I hear several footsteps running alongside of me. They stop running and those hands lift me up and put me back down somewhere, somewhere cool, and clean feeling. And they lift up my head slightly and open up my mouth real wide, and they place something long, and cold down inside my throat. And they're wrapping something tight around my head. And a male voice shouts, "Annie, can you hear me…nod your head if you can!" And I want to, but I can't, my stiff body won't let me. And they're tearing at my clothes putting sticky things on my chest and again, I hear that BEEP…BEEP…BEEP. That 5oo lb man is easing up off me now, I ain't feeling much pain anymore, and all I wanna do is sleep.

Part XIII

1986

CLIP….CLOP…CLIP…CLOP! I awaken to the sound of clipping and clopping clogs beating against the tile floor. I try to open my eyes, but through a blurry haze of pain I can barely open up one eye. And the more I try to wake up the more the pain and stiffness tries to take over. I've been here at this hospital for over two weeks now, and they tell me I was in a coma for nearly five of those days. And I have one doctor telling me I'll have to take stool softeners every day for the next six weeks because of my anal tears. I have other doctors telling me I'm suffering from something called post traumatic stress disorder. I have other doctors giving me medication for the disorder. I have a social worker trying to talk me through the disorder. And I have a parade of tests, and a prayer book of needles. And it seems like every five minutes they're taking me down for another test, and if they ain't testing me seems like they're poking me and prodding me, but the doctors say I'm making what looks like a speedy recovery, and that I can go home in a few days. They've even taken me off the I.V.

I strain and squint, and I make out what looks like a small, young man in a white lab coat with a shaved head hurrying towards me, and he's clutching what seems to be a rolled up pamphlet in his hand. When he reaches my bedside, he quickly curls up one side of his lip, and with his index finger he slowly slides the pamphlet across my bedside table. And Lord, Lord, Lord, what did he do that for? The pamphlet has a black and white cover and it reads, "Living with AIDS". It seems to me…it seems to me, that man has just slid a lid over my coffin. And he offers me his hand (a plastic gloved hand at that). I look at his face and then at that hand as if it's an alien's hand. And I scoot away from that hand and away from that face. And his lips are moving, but I can't hear nothing, see? Because it seems to me…it seems to me... that invisible fists are strangling, closing, and tightening both of my lungs. And the fists have started at the bottom of my diaphragm and they're kneading they're way up, tightening, closing, and strangling my lungs! And I can't breathe. And what they're leaving behind is as lifeless and flat, as an empty water bag. And the fists are squeezing their way up to my throat. And I want to open up my mouth so I can breath, but my mouth is wired shut JESUS! I CAN"T BREATHE. I need to breathe. And my hands are tearing and clawing at my throat. I can't see nothing, I can't hear nothing. I just know that I've got to get outside…I've got to get some air…I've got to breathe! And I jerk those covers back and I kangaroo for the door, with my hospital gown flapping behind me!

And I'm running, but I don't know which way to run. And I don't see nothing but the dark, cold tile beneath my feet, and a shield of white lights that lay in front of me. And just then I hear the blaring announcement over the PA system, "Attention, code yellow…5th floor, east wing, code yellow…5th floor! (patient eloping)." I see the steel double doors of the elevator to the right of me, but I can't wait on no elevator. I've got to BREATHE! And there's a red sign near the elevator that reads exit, and a door beneath it. I reach for the tarnished knob, and before I know it…BOOM! I'm toppled to the floor (and my ribs and my stitches scream and shout their rebellion) by two, dark uniformed guards, wearing latex gloves.

"I can't breathe," I try to say through the wires; "I can't breathe!" Their arms are tussling and flaying. My arms and legs are tussling and flaying. "I can't breathe;" I try to mumble to them again, with my face flat on the floor "I've got to breathe!"

And I hear the sound of rushing heels and the jingle and jangle of beating beads above me. "Let her go," says, the young, feminine voice, but the two men don't move. And it seems to me, that their grip gets tighter around my arms. She stomps her heavy foot, and repeats, "I SAID, let her go!" And you can hear the silence humming across the walls. And with a deep sigh the voice adds, "I'll take FULL responsibility." And with those words the two guards part like the Red Sea.

And I crawl and buckle for the door knob. And I feel a strong hand whip and jerk at my hospital gown. And I hear knees drop to the floor and beads slap to the floor. And I see, nothing but a sheet of white, pulling me and lulling me. And she holds me so close, and she rocks me so tight, until…I still can't breathe, but I ain't worried about breathing anymore. All I want to do is hold her right back, just as tight as she's holding me. And a welt of tears, stings and streams down my face. A welt of tears, that blooms and blossoms unto her stiff, white nun's habit. And I take in her incense, and candle like smell. And I want to evaporate into her smell. I want to melt into her blood, her bones, and her muscles. I want to leave my body and sink and swell into her body.

And a long, muffled moan starts at the bottom of my stomach and wiggles itself up to my throat and it flows and slips between my tongue, wired mouth and teeth, "OOOOOOOOOOO." And it seems to land somewhere between her habit and draped shoulders.

And before I know it, I start banging on this kind nun's back. And I want to stop banging, but I just can't…see? And it's not because I'm angry at her, it's because I'm angry at God. And with each pound I ask him, WHY…WHY…WHY? And it seems as if she knows this and understands this. And she slowly unhooks my arms from around her neck and she takes my fist and she rubs my fists, and she tries to heal my fists, with cool soothing hands.

And for the first time I look into her brown, comforting eyes, and I swear up and down she's one of God's Angel's, with bangs that shoot and curlicue from beneath her white habit, wireless glasses perch upon her thin, pointy nose, and her smile spreads across her face, like warm jam on toast. And a knowing nod springs and bounces from her head. "Hi Annie…I'm Sister Christa," she says, rising from the floor, with her Rosary beads, singing and swinging at her hip. She offers me her hand. "Do you think you can go back to your room now?" I nod sheepishly and press down on my lip. I take her by her hand and lift myself up from the floor. The nearby guards once again step aside, as Sister Christa leads the way.

If that Sister Christa isn't a life saver, I don't know what she is; she belongs to an order of nuns called the Daughters of Hope. And Lord knows every time she comes into my room she pours me a big ole glassful of it. Besides the doctors and my regular nurses, and the social worker she's the only visitor I have. One day she comes into my room with that habit of hers justa flying and her feet justa stomping. And I gather that the room is far too dreary for her taste, because she whips and snaps those blinds up to attention, and she twists around and Sister Christa eye pistols at me. "Is it true…is it true what I just read in your chart?" She asks, and her eyes are doing some non-stop blinking. "Is it true that you're moving back to your old apartment?"

"Yeah, it's true…why?" I ask.

She lets out a deep breath of impatience. "Because you're going to start using again, THAT'S why. You're one of the lucky ones Ann, believe it of not you are, through divine intervention you've kicked your habit (5 days in a coma). But believe me when I tell you, you will NEVER kick the craving." she says shaking her head and finger. "The moment you're back in that environment you'll start using again. And furthermore, that rapist, what's his name No-Neck? He's still at large. How can you go back there?" she ask with a hunch in her shoulders and a question mark in her eyes.

"Where else can I go Sister Christa?" I ask with a snap of my head.

"Towards your future," she snaps back. And her light brown eyes become scary eyes, blaring eyes, willful eye. And there's a long cape of silence in the room, a cape that seems to hold us and tie us, a silence that's finally torn by the siren of an ambulance…coming closer and closer. And Sister Christa seems to exhale her impatience and drops her shoulders and says, "Not your past. There's nothing back there for you Ann." And she blinks her eyes again and twists up her mouth and asks, "How does it feel knowing you're HIV positive?"

I always thought this nun had more sense than to ask me a foolish question like that. "How do you THINK it makes me feel? Knowing I'm caught between a hard place and a headstone?" and I look at that woman like she ain't got the sense she was born with. "Huh…how would YOU FEEL, Sister Christa?"

And she bounces those eyes and smacks those lips and says, "Hungry."

And now I KNOW I'm dealing with a straight up fool, and I look at her like she's riding the crazy train and I say, "What the hell is appetizing about death?"

And her hands and eyes wave with excitement and she says, "Not for death, Ann…but for LIFE! Let this make you hungry for life. I want you to stand at life's buffet table and taste everything you can! And when no ones looking, cram as much into your mouth as you can…I do," she says with a wink and a smile.

"You see Ann, so many people spend there whole lives waiting at life's doorway, afraid to go in, waiting until tomorrow…but My Mom always said that it was wait that broke the bridge down!" she says justa smiling and shining. And then she narrows her eyes and puts her finger to her mouth and asks, "What do you want for yourself Ann? What do YOU really want?"

I look down at the floor, because I never really thought about it. Sometimes we get so caught up on one of life's waves and we just ride it, and we forget we can always get off and star over and that we do have choices in life...LIFE! Ohhh, I tell you LIFE…ain't it something? Sometimes I see life as being a big ole baby doll, a baby doll you just wanna hug, squeeze and play with forever. But Chile, just like life, if you play with with that baby doll too hard and squeeze it too hard it'll wear and tear long before its time. And I finally look up and I look at that lil' nun, and I say, "I ain't got no money, but I would sure love to cut me a demo. I would sure like to see where it takes me."

And now she shakes her head and looks at me as if I'm riding the crazy train and she says, "Then do it Ann, for God's sake do it…find the funding, find the resources…do it," she says with balled up fists. I look at the floor again, and I nod my head. And she adds, "Let me do a little searching, but I think there's a half way house in the area, its run by the Sisters of Mercy, and they cater to HIV and AIDS patients. I think you can probably live there for awhile. And they can assist you with SSI and eventually…housing. Let me do some checking around, okay," she says with a quick nod and a smile. And with a twist of her mouth she says, "I have an old friend in the music business too…let me see what I can do."

And she takes her lil' spindly legs and heads for the doorway. And I sure hope her thin legs are strong enough, because I'm sure putting my entire burden and all my weight on this one little nun, she can't weigh anymore than a hundred pounds herself. And as that lil nun walks away, for a moment, just a moment it seems to me as if her habit stretches out, and spreads out so far, so high it's as if she has wings on her little shoulders.

Part XIV

1986

The washing…the rinsing...the stacking….the washing…the rinsing…the stacking… Mama sits at the kitchen table with her hand cupped beneath her chin looking out the window at the autumn night. And after nearly ten years Mama still has a curve in her hips and a swerve in her waist. The patches of time have made themselves a home on Mama's hair and face. And I can't help but to wonder is she really staring out that window, or staring deep into herself? Gloria, sweet Gloria stands at the sink washing our dinner dishes. And the only sound that's heard in this kitchen is the sound of the washing…the rinsing…the stacking.

I don't say nothing, Mama doesn't say nothing, and Gloria hardly ever says nothing, just the washing…the rinsing…the stacking. And then I see her, coming in from the shadows, Ghost Annie Mae, young Annie Mae, screaming Annie Mae, weaving, dodging the whistling and the sizzling of the slinging electric cord Annie Mae. And I look over by the stove and I see her sitting there, Ghost Annie Mae, young Annie Mae, wincing and shuddering Annie Mae, beneath the spider web smoke of the hot straightening comb that barely misses her scalp and then …burns and singes her scalp.

"What you come here for," says Mama, still looking out the window, snatching Ghost Annie Mae back into the shadows.

"Huh," I say, snatching me back into attention.

"You heard me," says Mama, still looking out the window. "What you come heah for? I ain't seen tail nor teeth of you in damn-near ten years. What you come heah for?" And somewhere between the guilt and conscience of my throat the words get all twisted up and gnarled up, and can't nothing come up... but phlegm.

I stretch my arms across the table and finger Mama's old knick-knack salt and pepper shakers, shakers that are as old as I am. And Mama jerks her knowing eyes towards me and bites down on her lips and the truth and says, "I know and trust in MY God that you didn't boogaloo yo ass up in heah to ask ME for no money!" And Mama curls her fingers to her mouth, and looks at me as if she ain't never seen before and says, "Lawd have mercy…guide me Jesus, guide me. You MUST think I'm a new kinda fool! Baby, wherever you left yo mind ya better go pick-it-up!"

And I still, can't say nothing. I just let go of the knick-knacks and let my fingers crawl into my lap, not looking at my Mama. Ain't no way in red HELL I can look at Mama. And still I can hear Gloria washing…rinsing…and stacking.

"Tell me Annie Mae," Mama says, pounding her fist on the table so hard the little knick-knacks dance and sway. "Tell me you didn't come heah trying ta fish through MY coin purse…TELL me?

"I…I…I," I stammer, looking in the back of my throat for words that don't seem to be there. I take in a big gulp of my shame and say, "I…I need $3,000 to cut a record demo. You're the only one I know with that kinda money."

And Mama looks at me with a giggle in her eyes and a smile on her face, a smile that turns wide, so wide I can see all of Mama's teeth and bridge work, so wide that Mama throws back her curls, quinces her eyes and lets her laughter ring throughout the kitchen, riding and sliding in and out the little holes of the salt and pepper shakers. And Mama becomes pop-eyed and let's out a "OOOOOH, Lawd have mercy!" And she lets out one more big breath, she shakes her head and with her hands patting against the air, she says, "Wait now…wait, you mean ta tell me you done spent the last ten years in the streets playing blind man's bluff with yo life, and now you gone prima dona yo ass up into MY house and try ta latch on to a piece of my life and a piece of MY coins? Bitch, you must be crazy! I'll bend down and kiss the devil's red ass befo' I'd give you one dime! That's why I tried ta give yo ass a good education so you wouldn't halfta face these kinda days…Bitch!" Mama dry spits (puh…) and she twists and turns up her lip, and pushes away from the table, as if I smell or something.

And Gloria finishes the dishes and turns around and wipes her hands on her apron. And she just stands there, not moving, not talking, just watching. And my eyes glimpse and glance over Gloria the way a man would. And I notice how the apron curves across her small waist and then fans out like a sea shell across her round hips. And I wonder how such of a knock-down beauty can choose to stay home with Mama, a woman with her master's degree, a woman that is now the vice-principal of an elementary school, a woman who's heels didn't just click-and-clack across the floor, but seems whisper and shimmy too-too-sexy…too-too-sexy. And I can't help but to wonder did she sneak and do-the-do at a hush-hush-rush-rush, lunch-time motel, when the only thing on the menu is good lovin'? Seems to me she should have dusted off her heartache a long time ago (the pain of her fiancé getting killed in Viet Nam), and gone on with the bizness of living and loving. Life is buzzing all around Gloria Jean and yet she refuses to buzz back…Gloria…the watchful one…the beautiful one…the mystery one. Did years of anti-depressants white wash her womanly feelings and cravings? Gloria catches my glances and I say, "Why don't you come sit down Gloria?"

She shakes her big head of curls and says, "No, thank you."

And Mama's voice stabs through the air with… "Get the fuck outta my house. You ain't welcome heah no mo."

"What," I ask, as if I've been doused with ice water.

"Is ya deaf Bitch, I SAID get the fuck up outta my house!"

And what did she say that for? I cock my head at her, I bubble my eyes at her and I let all the years of anger come zooming into her, and I say, "I ain't going nowhere Mama…you owe me," I say, pointing my finger against my chest, "You…owe…me!"

"Bitch, the only thing I owe you is a foot up yo' black ass," Mama says, real slow like. "Open up that back door Gloria, I got some trash ta take out." Mama says real quiet like, never taking her eyes off me, but Gloria doesn't move.

"You DO owe me," I hiss…"You DO owe me!" And I pound my fist on the table…so hard…until the table legs squeak like a mouse…and what did I do that for? WHOP...Mama slaps me so hard her bifocals falls off her face and bounces to the floor. And the side of my face heats and swells like boiled rice. And I lift up my face, my finger and my courage and I say, "You can slap me all around this house and all outside this house…if you want to, but that can't peel away the truth…you…owe…me," I say, with my fingers tapping on the table.

And Gloria rushes over to give Mama her glasses; she even adjusts them on Mama's face. And Gloria's cuts me a look and her narrow eyes seem to say "Don't push her." Gloria's twisted mouth seems to say, "Use some common sense." And Gloria's bunched up forehead seems to say, "Don't come here to act out." And I paper shred Gloria's eyes, mouth and forehead.

And Mama drops back into the chair like there's a heavy weight bearing down on her," and says, "How do I owe YOU?"

And with bitterness in my throat I say, "You left me Mama…you left me to fend for myself in New York. I woke up that morning and you were long gone…you didn't even bother to leave me a note."

And Mama looks at me as if I'm crazy or something. "Ahh hell, I left yo ass some notes alright Baby, dead president notes, and plenty of 'em, hmmmp. I betcha that much," Mama says, twisting her head and fingers. And Mama careens her head towards mine and with narrow eyes she says, "And then I turned around and wrote you a mighty healthy check to tied yo ass over until yo' grant money came through now didn't I? Ahh but you ain't speaking on that, now are ya? Speak God's truth Annie Mae, or don't speak at all. And on top of alllll of that," Mama says, fanning her finger, I left you a pamphlet for allll of the student housing. Didn't I…huh didn't I do it? Now sit there and say I didn't, and I'll knock the dog mess outta ya!" Mama says, with a shaking head and blaring eyes. And with a cunning smile Mama adds, "I thought for sure if you were grown enuff to cock yo legs open ta make a baby, you'd be grown enuff for New York City.

My eyes try to blink away Mama's last sentence. With a tilt of her head, Gloria's eyes bounce from me, to Mama and back to me again. "What good is all that paper Mama, it can't replace YOU?" I finally say, with straining eyes. And again there's a long silence. And a man's laughter from the street pours into the kitchen.

And finally Mama says, "How could I face you with a sober tongue in my mouth…after all the ugly things I said…how could I face YOU, daughter?" And the truth leaves Mama's lips and stretches itself upon kitchen table.

And my tongue smacks on Mama's truth and says, "And I've had to live with that UGLY everyday Mama, for the past nine years I've lived with that UGLY. That UGLY tucks me into bed every night, and gives me a wake up call EVERY morning." And I squash my face and say, "They say the Lord don't like ugly, but you sure do, because all my life I've been spoon-fed on UGLY!"

And Mama cackles like a witch, and hunches up in her shoulders, and swats at my words with her hand and says, "Well, if that's how ya feel Baby don't fight the feeling. Who am I ta change it? That's yo' bizness baby and yo toothache…not mine. You can squat down in one of life's pot holes if ya want too, or you can keep-on-keeping-on, because I guarantee ain't nobody gonna squat down in there with ya. They're gonna try their best ta swerve across ya and go across ya, so you just sit there in yo lil' life pot hole Baby if ya want to and watch life pass you right on by…hmmmp," Mama says, crossing her arms and shaking her leg.

Mama's vein on the side of her neck starts to swell, jump and flutter, and she says, "Ahhh ya wanna throw a pity party Annie Mae, well come ooonnn with the tissue Baby, because I sho' got some issues! Come on… let's throw it Baby! My phone number ain't change, and my address sure as hell ain't changed. What stopped yo abled bodied ass from seeing ME Annie Mae, huh…tell me that? What stopped you from sending me a rosebud of kindness? What stopped you from offering MEE a spoonful of hope? I JUST wanna know."

"How can I call a mother that says she wants HER child skeleton dead?!" I scream. So loud…so loud that time seems to echo, stop and freeze in that very kitchen."

Mama holds her breath for what seems like a long time, and then she cuts her eyes over at Gloria. Gloria seems to be looking anywhere and everywhere…accept at Mama. "Words ain't never hurt nobody," Mama says, real quiet like.

"Mama," I say, trying to push down my sadness, "Your words hurt me soo much, and so bad that my mind ain't nothing now, nothing but a hallway of pain, that YOU painted there Mama…that YOUUU plastered there!" I say pointing MY finger at MY Mama (what did I do that for?).

And Mama snatches my finger and twists and bends my finger. "Bitch…" Mama says with sparks of gun powder in her eyes, "If you don't get that finger outta MY face I'll BREAK it off! Do you hear Me?!" Mama says…and BAM…Mama slams my hand to the table like a wrestler. My finger throbs and hurts so bad, it's all I can do not to rub the damn thing, because, I can't let Mama know she has the upper hand...see?

Mama huffs on a big piece of calmness and says. "Now, I want you ta think Annie Mae, think about MYYY actions. Think about all the scrimpin', sufferin', and the saving I did for YOU and Gloria. Think about how many beds Iyyye had to make, think about how many toilets Iyyye had ta scrub and suds in order to give YOU a good education. Sometimes….I felt like I was scrubbing and sudsing away at my self respect!" Mama says, with slits for eyes and a slit for a mouth, and she drops her head and starts fingering her house dress and adds, "And when I felt like I just couldn't do it no mo' I'd clean those white folks furniture so hard, so bright, I wouldn't see myself in them anymo', All I could see was YOU…bright shining star Annie Mae, performing befo' Kings and Queens Annie Mae. MY Annie MAE! And what did I get for it…Huh…what did I get? A nothing…a pure-dee piece of nothing…a juke joint slut, that's what I get." And she curls up her lips and looks at me like I'm a dead street dog.

And Gloria finally opens up her mouth and says, "What you don't know Mama is that Annie Mae has had several write ups in the local papers. She's really becoming quite a south-side celebrity." And Mama shoots icicles at Gloria. And Gloria shoots her eyes to the floor, and curls her fingers against the edge of the sink…silent Gloria…watchful Gloria…trying to make peace Gloria…my Gloria.

I ain't near-about no fool. I got sense enough to KNOW when I'm trying to kindle Mama's fire. I KNOW I'm saying things to Mama that can land me bone-yard dead, but I can't help myself…see? The words are puffing outta me like a smoke stack "I ain't never asked you to DO nothing for ME! Anything you did for me, you did for yourself…never for me," I say with a shake of my head. And it clicks in my mind, like a combination lock, I remember what the doctor says before I left the hospital. He says as my condition worsens so will my mind. I think he calls it dementia. Is that why I'm testing Mama?

And Mama wears a twisted smile on her face and says, "Ya know what? You're right Annie Mae. You're as right as Church on a Sunday morning. I didn't do it for you; I did it all for me. What God fearing mother doesn't want their child to be fended for better than she was fended for? YOU tell me that?" And once again Mama's eyes spark gun powder, and her red polished finger waves like a warning flag in my face, and Mama says, "You better be mindful of WHO I am Annie Mae, and where you are."

"Nawww Mama," I say, seems to me all those years ago YOU shoulda been more mindful of ME. You wrapped allll your dreams around me, and alll your loving around Gloria. It seems to me I could have used a lot more of that loving and a little less of that dreaming."

And Mama's vein is justa pulsing and a throbbing, "You an ungrateful ass Bitch, you ain't shit! Do you hear MEE? You ain't what the cat left in the litter box. It took all my wits and all my strength ta get yo ass up in Julliard. And what did YOU do, ya got up there and showed yo natural-born ass. Now didn't ya? They wrote me, THEY told me how ya carried out…hmmp ya think I don't know? I know all about YOU Baby…hmmp." Mama says twisting her mouth and snapping her house dress.

And Mama starts to yanking, a tugging and a twisting at the hem of that dress. And for a long time she doesn't say nothing, she just sits there yanking, a tugging and a twisting. And finally Mama's veins starts to throb again, and she says, "I sat here and waited for youuu Annie Mae, waited for youuu in a corner called time, and when you do bob yo' ass up in heah, you bring HELL as yo' house warming gift. If I'd a known for one second you'd grow up and cause me THIS kinda heartache, Baby, when you were born I would've strangled you by yo' own naval string (umbilical cord)," says Mama, still twisting at her dress.

And I pop up like hot toast and I stand over my Mama and yell, "Ya want me dead so bad Mama, well, here I am, KILL MEEE!" I say, pounding my hand on my chest and justa stomping my feet. "KILL MEE! The last time I saw you, YOU wanted me skeleton dead, well here's your BIIIG chance Mama, kill me, and take MEE OUT! Finish it…finish what you started in the hotel room…FINISH IT!!" and my body, my face and my hair is justa twisting and a twitching, like I'm having a seizure, but I can't see Mama in front of me, I can't see NOTHING in front of me, all I see is a steel sheet of heartache. And the next thing I know Gloria is dragging me by my shoulders, trying to lead me to the front door. I jerk away and haul away and say, "Ugh…ugh let me go Gloria I'm tired of this!" I get ready to turn around and give Mama some more of my hellion pieces, and Gloria's eyes flint and dart, from the side, to me and to the side again. And with a firm grip and a frown Gloria tries to push me towards the door, I snap at Gloria and say, "Don't you push--"

Mama comes from in back of me with a powerful… WHOOSH…WHOOSH…WHOOSH…"I'll pick gravel in HELL! Befo' I stand up and let you fuck over me!" she shouts.

Mama has grabbed hold of the broom and she's whacking me with it. I hear another set of footsteps running up behind me. Gloria grabs hold of the broom in mid-air. "Don't hit her anymore Mama. Pleeeze don't hit her. She'll bleed…she has AIDS MAMA…AIDS!" And SPLAT…Mama drops that broom as if it has wings of fire.

AIDS…AIDS that hot, stinging word twists and clamps itself around my face, arms and back, and I try to push and bury my face farther into the carpet. All I can do is ask myself…why…why? Yes, I am HIV POSITIVE, but I don't have full-blown AIDS…not yet. I DON"T HAVE AIDS!

All of those hush-hush letters I have written Gloria, looking for a confidant, searching for a no-tell, won't tell ear. And now this heifer has sold me out like Judas sells out Jesus. And I'm being baptized now, baptized in a river of shame and served up the Communion of guilt.

I'm ready now; I'm ready to be beamed up. Beam me up Jesus, beam me up now. Send down your death Angel and beam me up to your celestial universe. Because you see, I can endure a thousand whippings and a million slaps, but I can't endure one glance of my mother's eyes, cutting eyes, judging eyes, blaring eyes, my daughter has the package eyes.

You see, I know something now, something I didn't know before, that isn't a broom that lies here on the floor, it's the TRUTH…my truth.

The truth is like a corpse see, you can tie it down and weigh it down to the ocean's floor, ahh but you can't keep it down. With the help of time and God …that thing will pop up and bob up and give away all of your midnight secrets (and you'll never see it coming).

My shame has me clothes pinned to this carpet, and above me I can hear Mama saying have mercy," and I can hear her plopping down on a nearby couch, like she's waay tired. "Have mercy," she says again, almost as a whisper. "The chile has brought sissy cancer into MY house Jesus! AIDS Jesus…AIDS…Hmmp…Hmmmp… Hmmmp."

And I hear another set of foot steps joining Mama on the couch. And I hear the crinkling of cloth rubbing against the couch. They whisper back and forth, for what seems like a long time, whispering that's as soft as tissue paper. And I am still too ashamed to get my behind up off this floor, too ashamed to even turn around and look at Gloria and Mama.

And Mama lets go of a long breath of air, and it sounds more like a moan than a breath, and after a long pause she says, "Guide me Jesus, guide me…Gloria, gone on in there and get the strong box." And she adds, "You know where it is." And I hear Gloria pass by me. And the hem of her skirt flutters against the back of my head. And Mama begins to hum, and that hum grows into a song, *"Precious Lord, take my hand, lead me on, help me stand ... "* And in my mind's eye I can see Mama rocking and a swaying. And I hear Gloria's foot step coming towards me, but they're slower now, heavier.

"Put it on the coffee table," Mama says to Gloria. And I can hear the thud and the clicking of Mama's kinda large, steel safe box. A safe she has had since I was a child. I believe Daddy (Gloria's Daddy not mine) made it for her. I hear the twisting and the flapping of the key and the lock. I hear the lid springing open. And there's apart of me that's springs open too, see, because I'm getting what I want…what I came here for…but you see, there's another part of me too…the part that feels so ashamed, so exposed. And I don't know if I can ever look at my Mama's face again. I feel as if Mama has gone and done a kinda mind biopsy on me, and she now KNOWS ALLL my inner workings…but much worse...all my inner failings too. And the shame in me is so strong I rub my face into the carpet once again, like I'm trying to rub away my shame. "Annie Mae, get yo' no-good ass up off MY flo'," Mama growls. I pay Mama no mind. "Annie Mae…I know you hear me…Annie…hmmp!*"* And again I say and do nothing.

"How much did she say she needed?" Mama asks Gloria.

"Three thousand," Gloria says.

"Have mercy…Guide me Jesus, guide me," Mama whispers again. And after a long pause I hear the snapping and popping of bills above my head, and that popping and snapping goes on for a long time.

"Count it again, make sure I got it right," Mama says to Gloria.

And again I hear the snapping and the popping, and after a couple of minutes… "It's all there, you're right," Gloria says. And I hear the sound of paper sliding across the table.

"On second thought, wait a minute," Mama says. And she lets out another long breath of air, and starts snapping and popping on the bills again.

"Heah," she says, and out of the corner of my eye I see bills flying above my head like magic carpets. "There's yo $3,000.000 dollars!" And after the money has settled and scattered all across my head, fingers and sides, Mama says, "Heah's another five hundred, buy yo'self a pine box…" WHACK! "You'll need one soon." Do you know that Mama baseballs that wad of money? She pitches it so hard it smacks dead against the wall above my head (my body jumps). And that money slowly slides down the wall and eventually spreads and scatters, justa scratching, and a cutting at my nose, cheek and lips. And for a moment, Mama's words seem to have power over me, hoodoo power, voodoo power, scaredoo power, words that criticize and prophesize, words that reach and leach at my skin, words that won't allow me to move.

And I finally break away from those clothespins of shame. And I sit up and gather up Mama's money (but not my dignity it's still on the floor)…my money. And now Mama's words do her bidding, they slap the tears out of me, tears that drip and whip from my face slide on down to the money and the carpet (pine box…you'll need one soon). I try to gather up the money as fast as I can so I can get out of here without looking at Mama, but my tears are working faster, faster than my fingers. And with the money bunched up in both of my fists I try to wipe my face and nose with the back of my hand. That shame and guilt rise in me like flood waters; they centipede from my finger tips, to my shoulders, and bite and pull all the way up inside my brain. "Put that money down, and walk up outta here," that shame says.

"Find another way to get the money, this ain't the way!" that guilt says. In the end I put a muzzle on my shame and my guilt, and I scramble for the money and the door.

Epilogue

1988

I have good days, and I have bad days. I have full-blown AIDS days. I have I wanna curl up and die days. I have wanna ball up my fist and fight days, ball up my fist and cry days. I have death bed days. I have doctors telling me, I don't have long to live days. I have I'm so weak I can't walk days. I have can't control my bowels days. I have throw up, spit up days…but mostly, I have lonely days.

This AIDS thing, only God and a microbe knows if I contracted it from Shady Grady or from a bad needle. Oh, but you see there's one thing I do KNOW, I KNOW that if you keep zooming down life's interstate paying no mind to the warning signs and the stop signs along the way, life is gonna sling, slam and bam your behind right into something! Sometimes, you can walk away from that something, but if you're like me…you can't.

And sometimes, when I'm feeling just right, me and my three-prong cane like to walk out in the cold, it does my head good to feel that cold air nip and whip at my face. I cram my free hand deep into my pocket and I let that wind do its do. It feels so good to me, it makes me feel alive, to me it's justa snapping and crackling. And I like to walk around in my neighborhood when the snow is just starting to lick at the pavement. Chile, for me it's a real sight to behold. And I see the elderly walking their wagging, shaking their little tail-feather dogs or young mothers carrying their little ones back and forward to school. And sometimes they'll nod their heads and I'll smile and nod back. Or sometimes a, "Good morning Sister, how you doing," will pop from their mouths. And I crinkle my cold cheeks and I greet them right back. And I watch the stir of my cold breath circle the air. That's the way it is on my side, the south side, the gritty side…but Lord, it's still my side.

But after a while my limbs start to tingle and I feel weak, and I head back to my little apartment (it ain't much, but it's mine). And it seems as soon as I put my key in that door, my AIDS jumps and leaps from the walls and it nits and picks, and pulls and pinches at my skin. It's been waiting there for me all along. And it's times like this that I grow thirsty for some sista heroin. And it seems like my veins start to throbbing and sobbing for that warrior powder. And that's when I grabble for the telephone and call somebody and anybody (I refuse to let her get a hold of me again…I refuse). And sometimes I call Gloria and sometimes I write Gloria. And she writes me back too, every time.

I'm on SSI now. I never worked too much, so I sure don't receive too much, but it helps, every little bit helps. And I've got me a Filipino nurse that comes in a few days a week. Her name is Tessie. She's a little ball of fun, justa peeking out the corner and waiting for the laughs to roll. And she's just as warm as buttermilk sitting in cornbread, with her sho nuf little self.

And I have a volunteer by the name of Adam too. He is a big Polish brusque of a something, with a reddish blonde crew cut. And he might be scary to look at, but his gentleness and kindness just bounces and pounces the moment that man opens his mouth. And he comes in and helps me with my laundry and my cooking, or anything else I might need done. And I'm so thankful.

Oh, I almost forgot to tell you that I have me a record contract now …I sure do! I sent my demo to New York, L.A., all over, but the man that responds is right here in Chicago. His name is Bert Bertram. He owns Howling Records. He says he named it after Howling Wolf, a sho-nuf righteous Bluesman. Its right over there on 20th and Michigan, perhaps you've heard of it? And do you know that he's a good friend of Sister Christa? And I guess she must have pulled his coat tail to my having AIDS and all, 'cause I don't think no other record producer would deal with a somebody like me. Knowing it'll probably only be a one record deal and all. I don't know what kinda favor that little angel (Sister Christa) called in for me, but Lawd it musta been a biggun. She sure flapped her wings for me.

Oooh I tell you, just knowing I probably won't breathe long enough to make another album stings, tears and paper cuts my skin. But this is the hand I dealt…for MYSELF…MYSELF! And I'm gonna sit here at life's poker table, and play it, and sometimes fake it, all the way through.

And sometimes, Bert will call me early in the day and with a tickle in his voice and he'll ask, "How you doing today, Ann? You feel much like recording?"

And I always wind up telling that man the same old thing, I'll say, "I sho don't feel like doing much, but I always, always feel like singing." And he laughs and his sweetness just gushes through the phone line. And we'll usually set it up for the evening. And my sweet nurse Tessie sometimes if she can, after working hard all day, and tending to all those patients all day, she'll back track and help me to the studio. Oh it's sad, but sometimes it takes a tragedy just to let you recognize the goodness in people.

And that Bert Bertram will have a handicapped van to come and pick me and Tessie up, yes he will too. And it sho does help too, because sometimes if I'm feeling real bad I can't do much, but sit in my red, velvet motorized wheel chair. And let that thing slide and glide me towards my ambition. I sho don't like taking it anywhere, but you see with this AIDS thing, I've learned that if you don't sit up, and get up eventually you're gonna give up. Because we all know tomorrow ain't promised to NOBODY and it sho ain't promised to me. And I've learned that life ain't nothing but a race. And I don't know about you, but I ain't in no hurry to get to the finish line.

And sometimes, when this AIDS thing starts really getting outta hand, I slam that bathroom door behind me, and I look at myself directly in that mirror, but you see it ain't really myself I'm looking at, it's that AIDS thing. And I smack my lips, I'll narrow my eyes and point my finger and I'll say, "Listen heah Mr. AIDS, you better listen, and listen good, now I know you're a smart something, and a sho-nuf strong something. Now I respect you, and I want you to respect me too. Now you want to live, and I understand that, but I want to live too. And if you keep acting up and flaring up, ain't neither one of us gonna get anywhere. So you settle down now, so we can both get on with this thing called life."

And ole Bushy haired Bert makes it sooo easy for me. That man lays down all of my beats and tracks, so all I have to do is lay down my vocals. And usually in the studio I'm able to get just about any song down in two or three takes, but for some kinda reason I ain't able to do that with "Half Mile From a Heartache". This is a song about a woman that knows her man doesn't want her anymore…he's found someone new, see? And it's just a matter of time before he tells her it's over. And every time I fix my mouth to get this song out Bert stops me, his sho-nuf smile melts into a crack and a scowl. "What's wrong," I ask through the mike.

He twists his mouth and shakes his head and says, "I'm not feeling you Ann. I'm just not feeling you at all." Now, what some of you may not know is that when a producer wants more out of a singer…he'll push it out. If it takes allll night, he'll push it out, shove it out and sho-nuf snatch it out! You see, usually behind every power ballad there's a power producer. And that producer will huff and puff until he gets that music down. And sometimes, they'll have a singer belt out one line over and over again until he gets the sound he wants. And before you know it, he's done that with the whole song, and he has to tape, patch and loop the song together…just like you would tape, loop and edit a movie together.

So before I go any further I start noticing that my temper is flaring up a little and my joint pain is flaring up too. So I just wanna get it right so I can get up on outta heah and get my behind in bed! Now, I wrote this song, so you would think that I would know how to feel this song. And sure enough I narrow my eyes and start thinking that I'm half-miling my damn self, I'm a half mile from a head stone. And I cup my earphones real close, I throw back my head real hard, close my eyes real tight , and I sho let my pain rise and my illness rise from my stomach, my diaphragm, my lungs, my mouth and I stamp my pain and stomp my anguish, and my fear of dying right there on that song.

And when I finish with the track I take in a deep sigh, throw my head back on the chair and I look over at Bert, and he hangs his head and his mouth is justa trembling. "Is that better Bert," I ask, through the mike. And I see that man through the glass and he won't say nothing, he just closes his eyes and nods his bushy head.

After the album ("The Blues for Annie Mae") is wrapped up, I let myself become a bouncing ball of worry. How can Bert circulate my album if I can't go on tour with the damn thing? I'm just too weak for that now. And they barely play it on the local blues station. But that man, God bless him, God bless him, "Leave it to me Ann," he constantly says. "Just leave it too me." Oh but it's so hard you see? Because that devil is knocking at my front door, and I know, I just know he's growing restless and breathless, waiting for ME to pay MY dues.

And one afternoon, a few weeks later, my phone is justa jingling and jangling, and I'm home alone, and I'm taking so long reaching it, I'm so afraid they'll hang up. And it's ole Bushy Bert on the other line. “Pack your bags Ann,” he says with that usual tickle in his voice.

“What you talking about Bert,” I say justa grinning.

“You’re going to Memphis young Lady. You are nominated for a W.C. Handy Award, for best new Blues artist of the year!” he shouts.

“Wha…What,” I say, grappling for a near-by chair. “But my album hasn’t received any real air-play. It’s not even on the charts yet. How the helllll did you work that one, Houdini?”

“Hmmm,” he says. “I told you I would work it, as long as the album is produced before the nominations, and it’s mailed to the judges that’s all what’s needed. And after this, believe you, me, you’ll get plenty of exposure and circulation. You’re on your way Ann.”

And what did he say that for? And before I even know it, I feel it, tears justa falling down my cheeks. “Ann, are you still there?” Bert asks.

And through a sniffle and a heave, I say, “Yeah…I’m still here Bert, and I want to thank you. And if I had a thousand tongues I’d thank you with each and every one of them.” And I hang up that phone, hang down my head and I cry, cry, and cry. And I close my eyes and I let my fist pound on heaven’s gate justa thanking God for bringing me thus far.

And before we go any farther, I don’t want you thinking that I made boo-koos of dollars from my recording contract. Howling Records is a lil’ independent record company ain’t much money in my record deal, at all. And when I finish paying for the musicians and background vocals, the only thing I have in my pocket is a hope and a dream.

And I don’t know if you know this or not, but the W.C. Handy award is nick-named the Blues Grammy. And it’s held every spring at the Orpheum theatre, right off of Beale Street. And I want Selma and Gloria to come with me too, I send them both invitations and I’m sure hope that stiff, fancy paper won’t wind up balled up in the trashcan somewhere, but that’s a chance I’ve gotta take, see?

And at the last minute I get a call from the Memphis Blues Association (I’m sure Bert had something to do with this), they’re in charge of the award show. And they need a fill-in for the opening act. Huddie Hutchinson was scheduled to perform, but it seems like, he’s on tour in Europe somewhere, so they want me…Annie Mae to open with Captain Good Sugar and the Time Travelers…me, Annie Mae! God sure has been good to me…hmmmp…hmmmp…hmmmp.

And I'm heah y'all, I'm heah on Beale Street, the Blues Mecca Street! And I'm walking across these red bricks, where so many of blues soldiers have walked before me. I know I should of let that cab drop me off in front of the theatre, but I want to get out and walk, see…just me and my three-prong cane. And ooh child, I feel them now, I feel the Spirits of the Blues walking besides me. Ain't too many people on the streets this early in the afternoon, but the shops are open and you see a few tourists here and there. But I just know come early evening these streets are jamming and cramming, with tourist and the hutti-gutti Blues music will be pouring out of the restaurants and clubs, luring and baiting people to come on in, and chill for a spell.

I can't walk too long without getting tired, but I tell ya, hearing my steel cane click against these red bricks means so much to me… And across the street I notice W.C. Handy Park. In the middle of the park (but it's more like a square, no grass, just concrete and benches) stands a statue of the man, justa playing his horn. And child, you just know that I've got to stop in there and give that man his propers. Hell, if it wasn't for him I wouldn't be here in the first place.

And sitting here on this park bench, I feel it rising and stirring again. I'm talking about the spirit of the Blues y'all. And I feel my Blues sisters that have gone before me join me on this park bench. And I bow my head and give them their utmost respect. And like me so many of them ate a slice or two of that hard-time pie. And since they were women a lot of them weren't really recognized. I'm talking about Memphis Minnie, Big Mama Thornton, and so many others. It seems to me that this bench is getting a little bit crowded with their presence, but hey, that's quite alright.

And I look up and I glance across the street, and I shake my head and get sho-nuf tickled, because I see a big, glittery sign that reads, Memphis Minnie's Restaurant. And Lord knows its waay pass due. That woman has been gone for over twenty some years, and she died with hardly nothing in her pockets. And I don't know if you know this or not, but many people give bluesmen the credit for electrifying the Blues, and not taking nothing away from those sho-nuf Blues stirrers, but Memphis Minnie did it years before they did.

They say she would have some throw down guitar battles with these men. Ooooooh, but what I wouldn't give to see one of those Chicago battles, at the south side Blues Clubs. Honey, they tell me Miss Minnie was a sho-nuf label hound. She would be Puccied and Guccied from head to toe, and she would spread her legs apart and get into her sho-nuf warrior stance with a twisted mouth, and she was guitar ready. And they say she looked like an iddy-biddy school teacher, but once she got the party started you just KNEW the only school she came from was the school of hard picks, flicks and licks and down right BOOGEY! And her fingers gnarl and her face snarls as her guitar screams out the low-down Delta Blues. And every time she'd beat them men down, and sent them to the dogs. All the men could do was shake their heads and smile; they'd been outdone again (by a woman). And it was all in good fun.

And who hasn't heard the song, *"You Ain't Nothing but a Hound Dog"*? But did YOU know that Big Mama Thornton recorded it first? And we all know that the "King" made big bucks off of that tune, and several other Blues songs he covered. And poor Mama Thornton only walked away with $500 bucks for all of her "foot up yo behind" moans, groans and growls (get a copy if ya can…it sho is something). And her version was number one on the charts for a while too. And she's another one of my Blues Sisters that died broke. And if you ever see a later picture of her you can see how the doping and smoking had taken they're toll on that sister. And Ms. Janis Joplin loved her some Big Mama so much so she did a cover of one of her songs *('Ball and Chain').*

And did you know that the Empress of the Blues (Bessie Smith) herself died so broke that she was buried in an unmarked grave? It took the kindness of Ms. Joplin (just before she died) to set things right. Oh but I love them, you see, I love them all.

Well, I've sat here and mingled with my Blues Sisters long enough. I better get on up from heah, I gotta make it over to the theatre for the sound check. But sometimes it makes me crowing mad to think that the Europeans had to ambulance in and give the Blues C.P.R. We as Americans were willing to let it die…our music…our culture…our history!

And I'm ready Mr. Handy; I'm ready for my Blues close-up! Back stage I put on as much make-up as I can to cover up my lesions. And I'm wearing a red suede shimmy skirt and a sho-nuf tight matching shimmy vest (and nothing underneath it Honey…you know I still wanna look good). And I'm here on stage with Captain Good Sugar and the Time Travelers. And I don't know if you know this, but the Time travelers are all white. And don't let NOBODY tell you that white boys can't git down with the get-down. These white boys ain't shucking and they sho ain't jiving.

And Captain Good Sugar is actually the drummer. And he sports these long Bob Marley dreds. And when the Blues Geist hits that man, it hits him hard, so hard his dreds medusa, shing and ling across his face, shoulders and chest. And with all that hair I don't know how he can thunder and storm on those cymbals. But Baby he closes his eyes, gets sho-nuf possessed and the sweat on his dark skin gleams and streams as he hammers down the Blues.

And I hear a lot of stirring out front, so I take a peek from behind the curtain (which is very unprofessional). And I don't see a hint of Gloria or Selma, but Honey, the Blues royalty has arrived. And Honey, these musicians know how to dress to impress. Half of 'em are decked out in their Ray Bans, their silver, gold, magenta, and some wicked cowboy gear. I spot the L.A. big wigs, Chicagoans, New Yorkers, and don't forget the Texas heavy hitters. And the balcony swells with fans and chatter. They're all down here in the Delta, to pay homage, and worship at the Blues altar. And I feel so humbled. All I can do is close the curtain and bite my lip. And I feel a tap on my shoulder, it's one of the stage hands, "Get in position," he says.

And the band has just finished warming up. And I speed over to my mark, and smooth down my skirt, and my hair. And those heavy gold curtains open up. And The M.C.'s voice booms across the theatre and says, "Ladies and Gentleman, introducing for the first time, Annie Mae Jenkins, with Captain Good Sugar and the Tiiiime Travelers!" And there's a thunder of applause. And we open with a song from my Album *The Motel Blues*. It's a sho-nuf sassy number, with a throbbing; gnawing at yo soul kinda beat. And the wrap-around sun-glass wearing guitarist smooches up besides me with a sexy sway to his hips and feeds me some intro, pot liquor blues. And all I can do is twist-up my face and dig in to this brother's low-down dish. And my hips are slinging to it and before I know it my mouth is singing to it. I throw back my head and wail, *"Stuck between a hard place and a pick-up linnnne. I'm strannndeed in a moootel out on highway 59. AAyyye gave that man gooooood lovin till the breeeaaak of dawwwwnnn. I woke this morning all my money aaaannnd that maan were both gonnnne!"*

"Take it to church Annie Mae! Take it to CHURCH! That's MYYYY Baby up there," I hear a woman voice, a voice that echoes and bellows through the auditorium. "I told y'all she's was gone be a somebody. I told y'all!" And it's Mama…my Mama…Miss Selma Louise Jenkins! She didn't let me down. And I see Gloria's smiling face in the back of the theatre. And I smile and wave back. And I go on singing (almost missing my beats). And Mama must be riding the Blues go round. Because her hips are telling me that she's finding the music grooving, her legs are telling me that she's finding the music moving. And Mama's arms are telling me that she's finding the music sho-nuf soothing. And I'm justa singing and gushing over my Mama. "That's my Baby," she says to an usher that tries to escort her back to her seat. "That's my Baby up there!" He looks up at me with a frown. I smile and nod and he lets go of Mama and nods right back. And Mama must be giving me a sneak-peek back into her girlish days, because that woman's body is churning, and sho-nuf burning. And the sizzling guitar solo comes in, and I shake and quake my way towards the edge of the stage.

And for a swipe of a second there's no one in that theatre but me and Mama. There is no music, no people, no nothing…just me and Mama and the hush that breezes across the theatre. And Mama stretches out her hand to me and I stretch out mine to Mama. And there's an invisible rope between me and Mama, an invisible rope that tightens and bonds us together. And I stare into Mama's eyes and she stares back into mine. And Mama's eyes speak to me. Mama's eyes seem to say, "Give it up Baby…what you holding on to it for…let it go…don't hold on to it, stop picking at your scabs…let it go!" And her eyes seem to bulldoze my pain and steam shovel my heartache. And they are taken and dumped into life's junkyard, a place where past burdens, heartaches, turmoil, and all forgiven wrongs MUST go. And with a glint and a grin Mama unthaws the moment. And the music, the crowds and the noise flood the moment.

And I'm narrowing my eyes and trying to throw it and sow it just as hard as Miss Selma, and we groove together, we shimmy together…ahhh we sho-nuf git-down together. And that woman is snake dancing her behind off. Do you hear me! So much so this white man from the Texas Blues scene joins Selma's Blues congregation and he's throwing up his hands and gyrating all up and down and around on MY Mama. And Mama lets him too! And all I can do is smile. And I look to the back of the theatre at my Gloria. The peaceful one, the thoughtful one, the kind one and I know she's the ONE that made this all possible. And I twist and shimmy my way back to the band and I finish up the song. And you know like any child, young or old I want to show out for my mother. And I give that song all I've got, I tightened up my butt cheeks, I stoop down real low, grasp my mike real hard and I send that song sailing and wailing its way home. "*AHHHHHHHHHH I Got da MOOOOTELLLLLLL BLUUUUUUEESSSSSHHHHHHHHHHHOWWWWWWWWWWW! YEAEEAAH!*" _Oooh I tell you, I tell YOU…I hold on to that last note child. I don't ever wanna let it go! And BOOM…! Captain Good Sugar thumps and bumps that last drum beat hard. So hard it echoes and zooms across the auditorium flies and soars above heads, looms against the rafters. And it touches down on the drumsticks and jumps right back into the Captain's fists.

And do you know that at the end of the song all the Blues royalty shoot up like bullets for me and the band (Me, Annie Mae!)? And some of them shake their heads, twist their mouths and narrow their eyes as their hands clap and roar for me and the band. And again all I can do is thank MY God. And the M.C.'s voice booms and says, "Welcome, to the sixth annual 1988 W.C. Handy Awards."

Afterwards, I limp out and join Selma and Gloria. And my mama…my mama squeezes my hand so tight. And bounces it up and down, down and up and says through a pouty mouth, "You turned it out Annie Mae. Do you heah me girl…you turned the motha out!" And even if I don't win a thing, her approval is my trophy. And my heart tingles and leaps. But you see, I'm thankful for the sort of dark lighting, I'm afraid of Mama detecting my lesions. How would she feel about me then?

And I try to hold my head down for most of the show, and almost as if my mama is reading my thoughts she lifts up my chin with her end finger and looks into my eyes and says, "No matter what you are, you're still MY child." I look over at My Gloria again; the peace making Gloria, the love seeking Gloria, the risk taking Gloria and again I know she's made this moment possible. And again my heart tingles and leaps.

I get lost on a street called happiness, so lost I forget about the awards, and the announcements, and Mama shakes my hand (and brings me back from that street), the hand she never let go of and says, "It's coming up now, Annie Mae."

And I'm up against some fierce competition. Competition I feel is much more deserving than me. These two other women and one man, and they're records are constantly played, they're constantly touring, and they've worked hard for this honor. And to be honest with you I feel as if they have far more talent than I do. "And the winner of the best new artist of the year award is (and again Mama squeezes my hand as tight as she can), Annie Mae Jenkins!" And the crowd roars and Selma soars. And that's when I realize that I'm too weak child… I'm too weak to move.

"Get up fool," Mama shouts, trying to push me up. "Get up!" But still I can't move. And Gloria has to squeeze over towards me and help me out of my seat. And she walks me half way down the aisle and she whispers, "Can you make it from here?" I nod and smile back. And the roar of the crowd is still going on.

And I hear Mama shouting, "That's my Baby. That's MYYYY Annie Mae!" And when I finally climb the stairs I feel so weak, I'm afraid I'm gonna tilt back and fall(with all of the excitement I forgot my cane and left it backstage). And I feel the strength of a strong hand, a hand that centers me and anchors me. And I look back and it's one of the ushers, and he flashes me a reassuring smile (the same usher that tried to lead Mama back to her seat). And I mouth him a thank you. And As I walk up to the podium the crowd is still roaring for me, cheering for me. And a tall, slender woman hands me the golden statue, of W.C. Handy playing his horn (the father of the Blues), and at the bottom it reads Annie Mae Jenkins, "Best new artist of 1988". And it seems so heavy; I place it on the podium with a hard thud.

And I catch my breath and I catch on to the podium and I hold on to it hard and heavy like. And a long "oooooh" is all that comes out of my mouth. And I look down at the audience, all of the musicians that I've admired and listened to for so many, many years. "Thank you," finally comes from my throat. "It's sooo many people I want to thank and need to thank tonight. So many of them that made this journey possible, but I mostly want to give thanks to the Heavenly Father who makes ALLL things possible. I would like to thank my mother, without me even knowing it she dressed me up for this very journey… so very long ago. I would like to thank a little nun by the name of Sister Christa who taught me not to be afraid of eating at life's buffet table. And I would also like to thank my producer Bert Bertram for taking a chance on me." And somehow the truth is snatching at my voice box trying it's best to come up outta me.

And I bow my head for a moment and clear my throat, trying my best to swallow that truth right back down. Oh, but you see like all truths it's too strong and it refuses to back down. And I press that podium as hard as I can and I say, "A few years ago, I would never have thought this was possible. You see, I was just happy singing the Blues at a local club every night, I was happy just to make enough money to booze it up and drug it up, that was good enough for me. And one day God sent me a telegram, and that telegram was the AIDS virus. And I sure ain't gonna stand here tonight and say nothing silly like I'm glad I contracted this virus. But it took this AIDS thing to make me realize how precious life is and how short life is. It took this AIDS thing to make me get up off MY bottom thing and do something useful with the time I have left. You see, this AIDS thing has taught me sooo much about life…about death…about headstones. You see, most of us see headstones as being a grim subject matter. But I don't because…because I'm only a hair strand away from one. You see headstones, are really a remarkable thing. There are eight numbers on each of them. The first four numbers are birth numbers…hmmp we didn't have anything to do with that. And for the most part, most of us don't have anything to do with the last four numbers either. Ooooh, but that slash…that slash right in there in the middle…we have EVERYTHING to do with that!" and I hang my head for a moment, and the theatre is sooo quiet Jesus…so catacomb quiet.

And I raise my head again and I say, "I'm one of the lucky ones. I'm able to stand before you tonight, but there are so many of my brothers and sisters aren't able to. Oh so many of them are gnarled up in a bed somewhere, and they look like they're starving to death. But you see, they're not starving to death, they're starving for life. And until science and the government put their heads together and their hearts together my brothers and sister will go on starving. I thank you; I thank you all for accepting me and making me feel welcome and a part of your Blues family…Thank You." I whisper. And I bow my head and again that roar, that lion's roar of acceptance pounds and aches at my ear drums. But it doesn't really sound like a roar anymore, it sounds like a flock of giant wings flapping…that won't stop flapping. I try to make my way back down the steps, and once again that nice usher, with the flashing smile is there to help me ("he's not afraid to touch me,'' I say to myself), "Thank you," I whisper to him…"Thank you for your kindness."

And Gloria, my Gloria runs to my side and grabs my award and helps me to my seat (seats that seem so far away). And I plop down beside My Mama, and she grabs me and holds me and I don't mean to, but I put all my weight against my mama. "Ooh you're sweating Baby, you're sweating something fierce." She says, with concern in her voice. "I think you should go to the hospital Annie Mae."

"Nawww Mama, I'm tired that's all. I just wanna lie down for awhile…I'll be alright." I whisper. And Gloria and Mama escort me outta there and back to the downtown motel where I'm staying. And do you know that Mama and Gloria take off my clothes and for a icy moment Mama looks at my needle ridden arm and up to me and back down at my arms. And she shakes her head and bits down hard on her cheeks, real hard. And for that one moment I know I hurt Mama, and I'm afraid that the pain will wash away all of the goodness of the evening. But Mama blinks her eyes and shakes her head again, real fast (like she's trying to shake away the pain) and she sings, *"And no matter what the crime, Lawd you know the child is mine."*

They bathe me, comb my hair, stroke my hair and tuck me into bed. And Mama's hands feel so good, and so cool against my skin. And all awhile Mama is singing to me, singing to me the first song she ever taught me, *"Zippity doo-dah…zippity aye…my, oh my, what a wonderful day."*

And Lord, Lord it has been a wonderful day, a blessed day, a I don't want it to end kinda day. And I don't know why, but I'm so tired, Jesus. And I just wanna lie here and rest a little while…that's all. And maybe, just maybe when I wake up we can go out and celebrate. Maybe, I can spoon down a little of those Memphis ribs everyone talks about. Oooh, but I'm so tired. And Mama smiles down at me and one of her long, thin curls dance and dangles against my cheek, I try to wrap it and loop it around my finger. But ooooh, I can't hold on to the curl any longer and it slips and slides away from my finger. I can barely keep my eyes open, I'm so tired…my eyes feel so heavy. "Mama, I'm so tired." I try and say. "Ma…ma (I mouth)"

"Shhh... Hush now…"says Mama, justa stroking my hair and still justa singing. *"Zippity doo....dah...Zippity...aye...my... oh... my... what... a ...won...derrr...fullll..."*

Printed in the United States
R3721100001B/R37211PG98181LVX8B/1-33/A